Not a Love Story

Samah

First Printing, 2016
Printed in India

ISBN: 978-93-83952-87-8

Editing: Roona Ballachanda, Wordit CDE
Cover Design: Wordit CDE

The Write Place
A Publishing Initiative by Crossword Bookstores Ltd.
Paradigm, A-Wing, 1st Floor, Mindspace, Link Road, Malad West, Mumbai 400064, India.

Web: www.TheWritePlace.in
Facebook: TheWritePlace.in
Twitter: @WritePlacePub
Instagram: @WritePlacePub

Dedicated to

Mrs. Meena Kirpalani

&

Col. Gautam T. Khanna

ACKNOWLEDGEMENTS

It has taken the belief, support and hard work of many people to make the dream of this book come true. I thank -

My father, Shailesh Visaria, for always encouraging me to pursue anything I wanted to, and for guiding me with his sharp business acumen. My mother, Gehna Mehra, who is the driving force behind this book. My penchant for writing stems from her. My second father, Bharat Mehra, for all the support and pampering. Vikram and Preeti Jasra, my beloved grandparents, for their love and spirit.

Shyla Jha for being an encouraging friend. Hardik Shah for his supply of notebooks to me. I've used them for this book. My friends, cousins and extended family. Many of them have inspired me more than they'll ever know.

Roona Ballachanda, my first-ever editor. Thank you for doing this with me. The Wordit CDE team and The Write Place team for making this happen. The whole Write India team at Times of India for encouraging writers to pursue their passion.

And most importantly, Anuj Bakshi, my partner in everything. His love and encouragement at every step of the way is my biggest asset.

CHAPTER 1

I'm instantly attracted to her. I feel something I've never felt before. Is this just the physical attraction a man feels towards a good-looking woman? I don't know, but I definitely want to find out. Maybe it is the grace with which she carries her simple, yet elegant *saree*. I'm a sucker for girls in *sarees*. Especially, yellow *sarees*.

She must surely be trying to impress me!

This couldn't possibly be true for the simple reason that we've never met before. This is the first time I've seen her, and ever since my eyes have set themselves on her they haven't noticed anything else. I'm sitting in a distant corner of the hall, slightly protected from all the activity around me. She hasn't seen me yet. Or has she? And man, am I waiting to meet her or what! I'm pretty sure I'm not the only one though. I can spot at least two guys ogling in her direction. It's quite possible that they're looking at one of the other girls next to her, but there's something majestic about this maid-of-honour of sorts.

Or maybe that's just for me.

Neha, the bride-to-be, comes out to the garden to greet people and seek blessings from the elderly. No doubt she looks splendid in her designer *lehenga* and heavy jewellery, but there's something special about this other girl, who's supposedly Neha's best friend. Something about her that I can't put a finger on is making her the centre of my attention at the moment.

Indian girls look their best in traditional wear, I conclude, and sheepishly move my gaze from her when I'm distracted by some family friend who greets me. After some boring chitter-chatter I'm by myself again and automatically try to spot her. She's talking to some aunty I don't immediately recognise, who is showering unnecessary love on her.

This girl will definitely have a number of prospective *rishtas* by the end of this wedding. With no actual logic behind my calculation, I estimate at least four, what with that breathtaking smile and captivating laughter that could make you feel like nothing else matters in the world. Although I've been working and living in the UK for the past few years, being born and brought up in India I'm aware of the age-old secret agenda of the *'rishtedaars'* to scout for suitable brides and grooms for their *betas* and *betis* at other people's weddings.

Although we haven't met before, my parents have met this girl on various occasions at Neha's house in the past few weeks, mostly to make earth-shattering decisions like the colour and font of the invitation cards, the décor, the venue for the various ceremonies, the menu for the festive meals, etc. about this wedding. My parents are best friends with Neha's parents.

I faintly recall my mother speaking fondly of this girl. If only I'd paid attention to her name when they'd mentioned it!

It's four in the afternooon now and just a couple of minutes before the ceremony begins. The function has been organised in a low-key but lavish manner at Neha's farm house.

The usual hustle-bustle of a typical *shaadiwaala ghar* in India has filled the house and it's almost as if the guests have been intentionally segregated age-wise. The children, stuck together like an army, are hanging around in the garden playing various games while some young teenagers sulk about, possibly wondering why their parents subject them to such outings. A few older teenagers and youngsters follow Neha inside to a huge room for some last-minute *masti*, drinks and photos. I, too, follow their lead as does my current object of affection, who is busy escorting Neha.

Within a few minutes, the youngster party is in high spirits, literally, some singing, some posing atop the glorious bed, some teasing, and what not. An informal rendezvous between the bride's friends and relatives, and their counterparts from the groom's side is about to take place. Jiya, Neha's younger and overexcited sister, silences everyone and shows her pride of place.

This is the moment I've been waiting for all day.

I can't help feeling excited. I feel like an adolescent boy who is being introduced to his first crush. The scenario seems perfect, like an opulent painting, or something out of a grand and cheesy Hindi movie. Except for one detail; one tiny, magnificent detail. I'm the groom.

CHAPTER 2

We finish with introductions from the boy's side first, but before we can start with the girl's side, a rather mature male voice summons us outside saying, "*Chalo sab bahar, mamaji bula rahe hai. Panditji ne kaha hai.*"

Everyone expresses excitement at once, with half of them barging out of the room as if a natural calamity has occurred. With eyes full of love and happiness, Neha looks at me, gesturing that we proceed to the function area. The pink of her *lehenga* looks pale when compared to the pink of her cheeks.

We're the only two people left in the room now. Suddenly, I feel a very apparent disconnect towards her. It's like I don't know her at all, which, in all fairness, is not entirely untrue. I stand dumbfounded and still, like a piece of furniture when she comes forward, holds my hand and says, "Come, let's go." The emotion with which she says this lingers on even after she's said it. That's when the actuality of things hits me.

Have I lost my mind? This is my own engagement to a girl I have myself agreed to marry. And yet I've spent most of this supremely important day eyeing an unknown woman. I feel disgusted, amused, embarrassed all at once, and quickly breaking out of my momentary stupor, follow the crowd to the main stage in the garden, Neha's hand in mine.

It's 4:30 pm on the dot when Neha and I make a grand entry on stage. It's not a performance stage or anything remotely close to that, just a slightly elevated platform to distinguish us from the commoners (guests) at the function. Indians have an unmatched way of putting the spotlight on the bride and groom and their families.

Everyone looks at us like we're celebrities; loud aunties are heard whispering to each other about the details of our outfits and ornaments. Naturally, we're the most important people at the moment. I just have to whisper that I need something. It could be something as basic as a glass of water that I am more than capable of getting myself, but the want of which shall send any Tom, Dick or Harry whom I've never met before into a frantic search. Of course, this worshipping will end as soon as the ceremonies are over and the same person who fetched me a glass of water as if I were dying may never look my way again.

As soon as we take centre-stage and seat ourselves, two exorbitant rings are served to us, separately. While my parents seem overwhelmed and overjoyed, Neha's seem humbled and teary-eyed. In an attempt to lighten the moment, Neha's maternal uncle makes a predictable wedding wisecrack. "*Last chance hai, Nikhil, bhaag jaa. Bahut nachayegi tujhe,*" he warns in jest and the entire crowd breaks into a guffaw as if Papa CJ is on stage. Neha gives her *mama* a nudge and blushingly silences her laughter. I almost consider her uncle's suggestion of running away and wish he were serious, but then I realise it's time. Taking the proffered ring from my mother's hands I remove it from its exquisite box, and in a jiffy slide it onto Neha's lean finger, instantly formalising our union. She follows suit.

There is a thunderous round of applause and unanimous appreciation at the choice of our rings. This is followed by a lot of hugging and kissing and congratulating. The two of us are made to take blessings from our elders.

Then the bar is launched and chafing dishes opened for those who want to indulge in this joyous occasion for the Ahluwalia and Bhatia families. Neha and I, along with our immediate families and friends move into the house to a more informal setting. A small party is to follow the engagement for those who want to let their hair down.

The ceremony happened so fast that I lost track of my *saree*-clad muse for a while. I am in the middle of a rather annoying congratulatory greeting when she appears again. After sprinting her way through the crowd she embraces Neha, smothering her with love and kisses. I just stare. Then she takes note of me, her best friend's husband-to-be. "Better take care of her," she threatens jokingly and sweetly winks at me, one hand of hers still resting on Neha's face. It's a wink I'll never forget.

Grabbing Neha, she then runs out of the room.

I don't quite understand everyone's hyper behaviour today. Do these festivities still really mean so much to people? Especially to women?

Moments after Neha's friend leaves the room, I find myself thinking of her again. What will she wear for the party, I wonder. Will she still look so attractive? If not, then it's just the *saree*. I should probably buy one for Neha and ask her to wear it for me. Yuck! That would be so odd. I immediately abandon the idea. This is all so bizarre.

It is 7 pm when I step down into the hall from my room, dressed semi-formally in a white shirt, blue jeans and a blazer. The living area has been converted into a makeshift party hall with bartenders, jazzy lights, a DJ console and the works. Everyone flashes me an ear-to-ear smile when I pass them, as if I mean the world to them. I join the kids who're having an intense round of an amateur card game to occupy their idle selves. All the menfolk are ordering their liquor and the women are joining the party in batches after their makeover of sorts.

I'm grabbing a beer when Neha walks into the room, with two girls next to her this time. 'That' girl is still wearing her *saree*. She's doing this to me on purpose I almost believe. But it's definitely something about the girl, not what she's wearing, that has me so mesmerised. I faintly recall seeing this second friend of Neha's before, but I haven't met her either.

Neha's looking nice too, I notice deliberately, guiltily, taking a big swig of my chilled beer. She's wearing a long and flowing western outfit in purple. Her friends literally deposit her with me and disappear into the room from which they had just emerged. They're probably going to dress themselves now.

Soon the room is abuzz with everyone assessing each other's outfits, and complimenting each other, and gossiping, and clicking pictures, and clinking glasses and basically indulging in different forms of revelry.

Champagne bottles are opened, toasts are made, and songs are sung. There's just so much going on in my honour and all I can think of is…**Aarti**! Her name is Aarti, I remember… triumphantly.

CHAPTER 3

"Good morning, fiancé." A voice that sounds nothing like my mother's disrupts me from my deep slumber. 'Fiancé', my inner voice replays the word in my head, instantly getting my eyes to open wide.

"Good morning," I reply, taking in my surroundings. Neha sits at the edge of my bed, dressed in a purple night suit. The smell of her *mehendi* is fainter. Thank God! I haven't warmed up to the 'fragrance' yet. "Did you sleep well?" I enquire.

"Ya. But not enough," Neha informs me. "Come on, get up and come for breakfast. Then, we're leaving immediately. Lunch will be at some *dhaba* on the way," she says, robbing me of my blanket. Then she leaves the room. I note that this is my first solo encounter with Neha as my fiancée.

The plan is that our immediate families and a few others will spend a day or two in Pune, which is a few kilometres ahead of us. It's like a mini vacation or extended picnic for both the families together for the first time. I wonder if Aarti will be joining us.

Aarti! This unknown girl who has majorly confused my otherwise untangled mind in a way like never before. As I head to the bathroom to freshen up I try to recall memories from last night; drunken, hazy memories. How pretty Aarti had looked in her plain white t-shirt and denims; almost matching me. She either wasn't prepared for the occasion or preferred being comfortable than fancy. Either way, her simple avatar didn't stop me from gravitating towards her.

I wouldn't say that she was the life of the party last night, but she had her moments and knew her Bollywood from her Salsa. We did do a jig or two in the company of many others, but we still haven't been formally introduced to each other. And now I want this more than ever.

I move down to the dining area for a breakfast of eggs and toast, and some world-famous *parathas* made by some unknown aunt of mine. Most of the house is done with breakfast and ready to depart. I quickly gobble some soggy toast and buttered *parathas*, and head up the staircase again to pack up and shower. On my way up, I overhear my mother discussing the plan of action with Neha's mom. Coming to the part that matters, Aarti **is** accompanying us to Pune.

I feel excited and then guilty for having felt excited. Kind of exhausted from feeling too many emotions at once, I decide to take a break from this topic and concentrate on the task at hand, which is to clear the room.

My best buddy Sid is also coming with us on our short trip. He's the only friend of mine who stayed back after the ceremony yesterday, and is in the room when I enter. We haven't gotten a chance to speak much since last night, but he is probably the only person who has noticed that I've been slightly aloof since the engagement.

"All cool?" Sid asks when I'm mindlessly putting my things away.

"*Haan yaar*, what happened?" I say instantly, defensively.

"You seem lost, bro."

"No ya, just tired," I reassure him, avoiding any eye contact. I can't let him get even a whiff of what's on my mind. However, I know that if I ever need help, no matter how absurd the situation is, I can count on Sid to understand me.

Sudden guilt fills my thoughts. I stress upon myself how I've just gotten engaged to a really nice girl, and on Day One of this lifelong journey I'm already going astray.

I proceed for a shower, almost hoping that it will wash away this 'dirt' from my mind. It's 1 pm when I'm out of the bathroom. Realising that I've overshot the time allotted for a bath, I speedily get dressed and recheck everything. This has got to be the most I've packed for a three-day trip.

The idea of being attracted to Aarti feels a bit revolting to me now. I'm hoping that during the trip she'll say or do something that'll totally put me off, and nip this growing attraction in the bud.

It'll definitely happen that way, I reassure myself.

In the next 10 minutes we're all set to leave for Pune. My parents and Neha's will travel together in one car. Another set of uncles and aunts will travel in another. A few cousins occupy a third car, and Sid, Neha and her two friends will come with me.

Neha, who now has the official rights to the front passenger seat of my car, sits next to me, demoting poor Sid behind her. Neha's BFF no.2 sits in the middle seat and Aarti right behind me, giving me full access to her face through my rear-view mirror. I'm convinced that this is God's very own Bollywood movie going on here.

Just as we sit in the car, Neha announces, "Guys, let me properly introduce you all. These are my girlfriends, Shreya and Aarti. This is Siddharth, and of course, Nikhil."

"Hi," we all say unanimously.

CHAPTER 4

One hour into our road trip and we're all in snooze-mode, possibly owing to a tiring flow of events over the past few days. I put on some music to keep myself alert as I drive. While others are busy tapping buttons on their phones, it's refreshing to see Aarti enjoying the breezy afternoon through her window. Soon we break our journey for a late lunch.

With all the cars parked parallel to each other at this 'world-famous *dhaba*', we place our orders separately, car-wise. Neha takes charge of the order for our car, the maximum dishes being non-vegetarian. Then she orders two veg dishes, and explains, "Aarti is vegetarian."

Hmmmmmm! A vegetarian? Negative points for Aarti. See, I'm an ardent Punjabi, and although I'm not obsessed with eating everything that moves, I consider chicken my birthright. I've grown up eating some amazing chicken dishes made by my mother and I would want to have a partner who can enjoy all sorts of cuisines with me, the world over.

This round goes to Neha, I assert in my head. I'm now on an unbidden mission to prove to myself that Neha is the perfect choice for me. And I'm positive that I'm attracted to Aarti only because I'm not supposed to be. She's the forbidden fruit of my life at this point and it's just a psychological defence mechanism that my mind is confusing me with. Maybe this is why people fear commitment. I'm only drawn to Aarti because I'm not allowed to be, I reassure myself.

"Chatterjee, you want some?" Shreya asks Aarti, offering her some of our butter chicken. Aarti refuses it.

"I thought you're a vegetarian?" Sid asks, mirroring my confusion.

Before Aarti can clarify, Shreya answers on her behalf. "This *natak* of hers is very recent. I'm sure she won't last a month without non-veg," she teasingly challenges Aarti.

"You'll see," Aarti retorts.

Aarti Chatterjee, a Bong girl. Why is she a vegetarian, I wonder. I want to ask her but can't bring myself to.

We resume our journey immediately post lunch.

The rest of the day goes by pretty normally. By the end of the day I've learned a few things about my fellow passengers.

Neha loves to narrate stories. Some of her narratives were pretty interesting and funny. Shreya has a bigger appetite than mine, and that is not a small thing to say. Sid is very awkward in the company of new female friends. And Aarti….. Aarti speaks less and laughs a lot. And boy, what an infectious laughter she has!

...

It's 10:30pm and we're all heading to our rooms, retiring for the day after a buffet dinner in our 4-star guest house.

Though the original plan was to dine at one of the popular city eateries, nobody was really up to it when we reached, so we decided to dine in and leave the city exploration for tomorrow. I've come to Pune after a really long time and I've heard there are a lot of new places to try out.

Now it's just me and Sid in the room. I must ensure that I carefully guard my secret. Poker face is now on. Trying harder than usual to be normal I say something predictable to Sid. "So…Shreya or Aarti?" A huge grin is painted on my curious face.

Obviously getting what I mean, Sid replies, "I'll tell you tomorrow. Need more time to think." He's grinning back.

Lucky for me, Sid is too tired to be chatty and falls fast asleep within minutes of our conversation, leaving me and my thoughts of Aarti uninterrupted. I don't exactly remember at what point, but I too doze off soon after him.

…

The beep of a text message wakes me up. It still feels like night but my phone tells me otherwise.

"Wake up. Breakfast time." Neha's message reads. The bed next to me is empty. Sid comes out of the loo, looks at me and says, "Aarti."

What? Does he know? How does he know? There is nothing to know. I don't love Aarti. Love????? What is going on! Did I talk in my sleep? How could he know?

A thousand thoughts flash through my mind and the horror is reflected on my face. I'm really confused. Poker face is now off.

Probably puzzled by my odd reaction, Sid squints and says, "Dude, I choose Aarti. I think Shreya's hotter, but not my type. I like Aarti."

Oh, that's what he means! I'm so relieved in a way that this wasn't about me, but irrationally, I don't like something about Sid picking Aarti. Sid is like a brother to me, but I don't like it. Nevertheless, giving him an approving nod and a wicked smile I get out of bed. It's time to start the day.

CHAPTER 5

"Goodnight, sleep well," Neha whispers in my ear outside her door, planting a quick, loving peck on my cheek. Maybe I should reciprocate? After all, we're getting married, and my gold engagement ring has licensed me for PDA. But with all the commotion in my head I just can't bring myself to fake it.

Giving Neha a boyish hug I escort her into her room with a gentleman-like smile, before leaving for mine which is one floor below. On my way down, I categorically analyse Neha's kiss and how I feel about it.

See... I'm just about like most other guys. And I can tell you something about us; we love girls. So I would be lying if I said that being kissed by Neha was something I didn't like or was repulsed by. But there is no doubt that Neha and I lack chemistry. She's pretty good-looking and we're both grown-up individuals, happy, healthy and fairly successful in our careers so far. Moreover, we're just two months away from getting married to each other. Our romance should be peaking at this point.

Gradually, I realise something. It's not just about this whole involuntary attraction to Aarti anymore. Why aren't Neha and I enjoying this phase of our lives to the fullest? Aarti or no Aarti, this should be the best phase of our lives together.

Then, why isn't it? We have complete independence, our parents' blessings and, most importantly, marriage is something we're both really looking forward to. Then why are things so lacklustre? Of course it isn't terrible. We're not sad or suffering. We're just 'normal'. Mediocre. **Why?**

Having witnessed arranged marriages pretty closely, I've seen how exciting the period before the wedding can be for a couple. Rohit *bhaiya*, my paternal cousin who lives in the neighbouring flat was wedded five years ago to my uncle's school friend's daughter. Frankly, his pre-wedding phase was pretty annoying for me personally. His Romeo-like behaviour knew no bounds. From helping him break into Nikki *bhabhi's* house at obscene hours of the night to delivering useless cheesy gifts at her office and home, my cousin, Ria, and I had to do it all. My own parents also had an arranged marriage. The thought of them romancing like this is nauseating though!

"Duuuuudeeee," Sid's voice raids my thoughts as I enter my room and shut the door behind me. "What a day bro! Actually, what a night! Shreya is too good. Even Aarti looked killer, but Shreya man! I like her. Shreya *pakka*. Final," he finishes, promising me.

'**Killer**' I agree in my head. Aarti did look gorgeous tonight. Not in her usual unconventional, arty-farty way. She was full-blown-commercial-party-good-looking tonight in her long, green gown. Green is a colour I truly detest. To floor me in a yellow *saree* is very easy, but to do that in anything remotely green? Hmmmm.

Neha was also wearing something similar in black. As usual she was well turned out. And Sid's assessment of Shreya isn't wrong. Shreya is like the typical hot girl we see in Hollywood movies. She's tall with sharp features and a great body, and she's always perfectly dressed. Her hair is never messy. Her make-up is never off. But she's nothing like a Hollywood badass by nature. In fact, she's naturally funny and can make intelligent conversation with anyone around her. Tonight she wore a fitted red dress that proved that she definitely goes to the gym. We'd all gone to a nightclub in the main city. No points for guessing, I'm still mesmerised by Ms. Chatterjee.

After a short chat, Sid and I decide to call it a night. I'm still a little drunk, and comfortably tucked into my bed. It's now assessment time.

...

Our day began early this morning. Everyone met for breakfast at 9 am. Buffet was on till 9:30, and no matter how rich or tired you are, you can't miss a complimentary buffet, can you? Everyone unanimously agreed on how refreshed they were when they woke up today. I, for one, have never experienced this. No matter how early I sleep or how rested I am, I can just never wake up and want to jump and dance. I always wake up in denial.

Aarti came down for breakfast in a pristine white *kurta* which she wore over a long red skirt. I observed her in great detail. So beautiful her big, expressive and always-lined-with-*kajal* eyes are. She uses them quite animatedly in conversation. Small silver earrings circled her tiny ears which are almost always hidden behind her hair. Her hair! She has straight, long and absolutely gorgeous hair, and I had the urge to smell it more than once during breakfast. She was wearing a very small, almost unnoticeable nose ring today. It made her look mature, but still very beautiful. I've never automatically noticed such minute details about Neha.

Over the days I've started feeling more and more strongly towards Aarti. It may seem like a very superficial thing to someone else but only I know how intensely I feel for her. I just want to get to know her so much, be friends with her. I had decided in the morning that before the day would be over I would break the ice with her. Not in an introductory manner, because that had been done, but on a personal, one-to-one level. There's nothing wrong in wanting to be friends with someone, so I harboured no guilt for wanting to befriend her.

Sid and I were the first two to reach the buffet table from our entire group. When Aarti came, Neha and Shreya were also with her. Out of exaggerated courtesy, Siddharth, who was sitting next to me, stood up to address Neha and offer her what was rightfully hers– the seat next to me.

"*Bhabhiji please, aiyena*," he said with folded hands and animated humour inviting her to sit beside me. Neha playfully admonished him for the mock teasing, and grinningly, she took the vacated spot next to me. God! Marriage is making me important. There was a time when girls only sat next to me when they were being punished by teachers, after being separated from their actual friends.

So consequently, Sid went and sat next to Aarti in very close proximity. The bastard! Everyone ate as if this were their only meal for the day; everyone except Neha, who ate a bird's breakfast. I'm assuming she's eating fixed portions nowadays in order to reach her wedding-weight target. Aarti surprised and impressed me with her appetite though. I love girls who love to eat.

Post breakfast we did some pretty boring activities like visiting people, jewellery shopping, clothes shopping, shoe shopping, *mithai* shopping, kitchenware shopping, which could easily have been avoided. Somewhere in the middle of all this unnecessary shopping we paused for a quick bite of the most famous street food of Pune. I did have some interest in what Aarti was buying. She didn't seem like a spendthrift, but you can never judge a woman's abilities to shop based on one experience. Believe it or not, I liked **everything** she picked. I'm not sure if I genuinely liked it at first instance or because she had picked it, but I liked it.

After the merciless shopping spree we all settled down at a nearby multi-purpose mall which was our venue for a late lunch. I was too full from the delectable *bhakarwadi* that my aunt always makes us have when we are in the city. Unlike most other Indians living abroad, I never shy away from eating roadside food when I am back here. Having grown up on the street food of Mumbai, my immune system is accustomed to it and I would like it no other way.

The ladies all sat huddled-up with the shopping bags in one corner of the food-court. Though a lot of the stuff in those bags was for me, the only things I had actually bought were umpteen packets of Shrewsbury biscuits. I love these. Even though the famous shortbread back in the UK tastes just like these biscuits, I never actually end up buying those during my weekly grocery shopping.

As the women went about reassessing everything they'd bought, showing it off to each other and doing some non-professional accounting of their expenditure, the men went and placed orders for their respective counterparts at the various food franchises sprawled across the vast hall. Aarti went to get her food herself. At this point, not only was I immensely attracted to her but also quite impressed with her.

After lunch, half the people went back to our guest house for some shut eye. The rest of us decided to accompany Aarti into a perfume store, where she planned to buy her father a gift for his upcoming birthday. This was the highlight of my day. Sid and I were busy minding our own business, testing perfumes we very well didn't intend to buy, when Aarti came up to us with two of my favourite perfume brands and asked, "Which one?"

"Need to buy one for my dad. I like both. What do you guys prefer?" she said sticking her tiny wrists towards me to whiff the tester spray and compare. "Paco," I gave my opinion and smiled. Sid said nothing. "Cool, thanks," she smiled and headed to the cashier.

So I'd been shopping with Neha a couple of times in the last three weeks, not by choice of course. But when you're about to get married there's so much that you apparently HAVE to buy. It's as if you were living like a homeless person before. During these three or four outings Neha always knew what to buy, what was the perfect price, the perfect colour, the perfect fit. I appreciated that. I thought I liked not being bothered by trivial questions like 'Which one is better?' 'What suits me more?' But oddly, today, I liked that my opinion mattered to Aarti. It's like she acknowledged that I had better knowledge about men's perfume than her.

Am I going insane? Am I finding reasons to like her? Well, I already do like her. That much is established. And I've officially lost it. I'm getting into such random details and it's all irrelevant at this point. She's my fiancée's best friend for chrissakes!

Anyway, the evening was quite relaxed. The senior generation left us youngsters to be by ourselves as they went visiting some more people. You see, my mother had spent a good chunk of her formative years in this city and my aunt is married to a Maharashtrian here, so we know a lot of people in the area.

Our plan was to drink up and party away. The nine of us (cousins included) were pretty excited about getting smashed after spending the last seventy-two hours with so many new people. Sid and I stuck to whiskey like we did on most occasions. Shreya drank wine for the apparent health benefits it had when compared to other alcohol. Neha, who generally drinks vodka, also opted for wine for reasons similar to Shreya's. Aarti, who confessed to having a few lousy experiences with vodka, delighted herself with rum.

Presently, thoughts of dancing with Aarti at the club fill my mind again. In my semi-conscious, semi-intoxicated state I imagine her in place of Neha. How would it be if I were engaged to her? I allow myself to imagine doing the ceremony with her, going shopping with her, sitting next to her for everything. I imagine her giving me the kiss instead of Neha.

My eyes flick open widely at the thought. Despite my drunkenness I will myself to think rationally. This is not reality. It cannot happen. I remind myself repeatedly. My only reality at this moment is a TV in front of me, a snoring Siddharth next to me and a shiny, expensive ring on my finger.

It's another moment of realisation for me. I've understood two very important things at this point. 1) I really want Aarti. 2) I cannot have Aarti. After much deliberation I make a decision in my mind. It's time for the three golden words….. Must. Tell. Siddharth.

CHAPTER 6

It's the next day when I'm woken up by a call from an unknown number.

"Hello. Yes?" I receive it groggily.

"Good morning, it's me. Come for breakfast, it's nine fifteen already," a predictable voice speaks.

"Morning," I can only bring myself to say. Even though it's nice of Neha to save my breakfast expenditure I can't bring myself to appreciate this alarm-clock type behaviour of hers. I do realise that my irritation is irrational.

"See you in 10," Neha confirms.

"Yes. Wait. Whose number is this? What happened to your phone?" I inquire.

"Oh, this is Aarti's number. You know what? My phone isn't ......" My brain stops processing the words after Neha tells me that she's calling from Aarti's phone.

All listlessness has suddenly left my body. I've got **Aarti's number.** I want to jump out of bed and do a victory-dance, but of course, I won't.

"Be down in 5," I say and hang up. I sit up in bed and reflect on my decision to confide in Siddharth. A decision I made in a semi-conscious state last night that still makes sense to me now. The onus will be on Sid now. I'm depending on him to either talk some sense into me and change my mind about this or completely understand and support my feelings. Yes! Telling Sid is the best option I have right now. Maybe he'll change the way I feel about this.

Sid comes out of the bathroom and after my quick turn inside we go down to break our fast. Owing to last night's merry-making no one from amongst the nine of us has woken up early enough to bathe before breakfast. Shreya and Neha are done eating when we reach down, while Aarti seems like she's just getting started. The items on her plate seem like they are at war with each other for the lack of space. She looks like the human version of an utterly cute pig as she eats in her pink night shorts and a two-sizes-too-big t-shirt. Can't I just grab her and go back to sleep?

Today, we are all heading back to Mumbai. After breakfast everyone decides to pack up, get dressed and leave as soon as we're all ready. Lunch will be in the main city after which we'll hit the expressway non-stop until home.

"*Yaar*, I'm still damn sleepy. Wake me up in an hour," Sid says as we sit in our room. I know that if I intend to tell Sid about my inappropriate feelings for Aarti and all my other new issues, now is the time to do so. Once we leave I won't get such a good chance to speak to him privately and seriously. But at the same time I'm petrified of his reaction; so petrified. But however extreme Sid's reaction will be, it'll be the mildest of all if I compare it to how my parents or anyone else will react. Whatever ensues after I tell him will only be a mild glimpse of what I should expect from my family. This is going to be difficult and awkward. But it's for the best. It'll make things better, I remind myself.

I start thinking of ways to keep Sid from sleeping, and more importantly, ways to broach this topic. How do you tell someone that you want to detach yourself from a partner that you had whole-heartedly agreed to attach yourself to, after your parents had painstakingly found them for you, fulfilling your every condition? And all this only so that you can attach yourself to their best friend!

"I like Aarti." The words are out of my mouth before I can control myself from blurting out my thoughts.

Siddharth turns towards me, completely alert, and giving me a confused expression he says, "Ya?....Ya. She's cool. So is Shreya. Seems like they've known Neha for long."

That's not what I mean. I **'like'** her; more than Neha. You're my best friend. Don't you get it? It's normal; it happens, I want to say but obviously don't.

I have to say **something**. You can't just make such bizarre statements in mid-air and leave them hanging. I don't know how to follow this up. I swear I just stare at Sid for the next whole minute as he flashes me his most baffled expression to date.

Wow! This is way more awkward than I'd reckoned. I've practically grown up with this guy. Over the years we've faced many situations that would be weird between people but weren't between us. From learning about the birds and bees to witnessing each other's parents fight we've been through it all. And yet I'm unable to do this with even a modicum of ease. We're not accustomed to confrontations or confessions. I think as a natural thumb rule, most guys don't discuss very personal things in detail. At the most, one will 'state' a fact if it's important, the other will 'acknowledge' it and they'll both move on to the next topic. There isn't much brouhaha over every little thing. But I realise that in this case merely stating and acknowledging won't happen. I'm going to have to try really hard in order to get my point across, if there is any.

"Bro, I really like her," I try to explain myself again.

"*Haan* okay. I get it..... *Kya bol raha hai*? Still drunk or what?" Sid fails to understand me again.

Awkwardness meter has maxed out. I can't believe how difficult it is to say this without being judged. And this is just Siddharth I'm talking to. There was only one other time in our friendship that I felt extremely uncomfortable in his presence. It was the first time I'd visited his house years ago. While we were eating lunch at his dining table his mother had 'accidentally' let out a huge thunderous burp in my presence. Believe me it was a burp like no other I had witnessed. It easily lasted over five seconds, I kid you not. If someone had told me then that she took lessons to master the art of burping, I would agree. If I remember correctly it even sounded like it was in a tune. And that was not even the worst part! After the roaring release she washed her hands in a bowl of water. Now that was normal, **until** she drank the water in that bowl in which she had just rinsed her hands. Yes, you read that right. She **drank** it! I learnt later and I cannot tell you how, that this was not an uncommon practice amongst

Gujarati womenfolk and it is considered beneficial, how icky it seemed notwithstanding.

That incident was excruciatingly awkward to endure. More so because Sid and I had just become friends. We avoided eye contact for days in school after that. But soon we grew out of that odd space. I'm sure there must have been a hundred other funny and weird things that might have happened to us but I knew that nothing could be too awkward for us after that. I was **so** wrong. That was a cake walk compared to this.

"*Yaar, sun meri baat,*" I begin again calmly. "Hear me out first. It's really not a big deal, so chill. I think I...."

"What!!!" Sid interrupts me with a sharp shrillness in his voice.

My calmness is short lived. Panic rises in my whole body as sweat beads trickle down my spine. Has he got it? I'm such a bunch of nerves at this moment.

"Ya, bro," I say shakily, wearily, as we both try to read between the lines.

"Sick, Nikhil! She's your fiancée's best friend!" he says with a smirk.

Okay, that was easy. I'm so confused by Sid's reaction. Why isn't he panicking?

I stay mum, hoping and expecting that Sid will say more.

"*Abbe saale ab toh sudhar ja...* You're getting married now. All this won't do. But Aarti is pretty cool *haan*. I can understand. Allowed *hai*. But listen if Neha finds out *na* you'll be screwed. Girls can't stand it if their boyfriend finds their best friend hot…. And don't ever eye Shreya okay. She's mine," Sid warns me playfully.

Damn. So Sid has only partly got my point. I think he thinks that I find Aarti attractive and that's about it. That's what I'd thought initially, until I realised that not only do I find her very attractive but I'm also very attracted to her. There's an extremely fine and important difference between the two things.

Anyway, I can't let the topic subside before conveying the whole truth to Sid. The window has opened for me. I must continue. I will myself to continue talking in order to make Siddharth understand the intensity of my feelings and of this situation. Before we leave I have to tell him about my unplanned idea of somehow cancelling this wedding and somehow starting an affair with Aarti.

CHAPTER 7

"Sid bro, *tu samjha nahi*, she's damn hot but that's not what I'm trying to say, I…." words fail me. This is so embarrassing.

"What **are** you trying to say, Nikhil?"

Just say it plain and simple, I tell myself. It's now or never.

"I'm having second thoughts about this marriage," I say far too quickly.

There it is. I have put these horrid words out of my mouth and somewhere into the universe. My journey to end something has begun, although I'm not sure how things will end. Right now I'm not sure of anything, not even if I truly want this or if it's some sort of distraction. Anyway, the words have been spoken. The ball is in Sid's court now.

Another whole minute of creased-brow staring passes. Sid and I have never encountered such a situation before. Not even as spectators. Some of our close friends have taken the plunge but such a circumstance hasn't ever arrived. Good for them.

"Abbey," Sid breaks the deafening silence. "Chill, chill," he says, relaxed as ever.

I give him a questioning look. I am confused. **I** don't want to marry my fiancée and the main reason behind it is her **best friend,** and **my** best friend wants me to **'chill'**???? Really?

"You're getting cold feet bro…. *Zyada soch mat*. It happens with everyone."

Oh, this is slow death! Will it be **this** difficult to convince everyone? Will everyone think they know how I feel, better than I do? I've a good mind to abandon this topic but that'll only put me out of my misery temporarily. I can't stop now. The ice on this embarrassing topic has been broken. I just have to vomit it all out till Sid realises how serious I am. And then, I kind of need and expect him to convince me that this is not how I feel. The irony!

"Siddharth!" Full names are for serious discussions. "It's not cold feet. I'm not scared of commitment. I'm ready for marriage. But not with Neha I think… I'm sure. *Kuch toh problem hai yaar*. I mean… There's no problem with her. It's just us. As a couple… I don't know… I'm damn tensed." This is as clear as I can manage to be at the moment. Come on! I've spelt it out for Sid. If he doesn't get it now, then communication is officially not a 'guy' thing.

"Huh?" he breathes. "Okay and what were you saying about Aarti? What is all that about? Does this have something to do with her?" Finally I think he's getting my drift.

I try to filter my thoughts before verbalising them but speaking is just too automatic right now.

"Maybe. See that's a separate issue. I really like her. But apart from that. I mean… If you keep her topic aside, I feel Neha isn't the one for me." I feel guilty and senseless even as I say this. It's so difficult to articulate things at times. "Or I'm not the one for Neha," I correct myself in order to be fair to her. Well, ironically.

"*Haan,* this is cold feet only, *mere bhai.* Today it's Aarti, tomorrow it'll be someone else. You're just getting nervous. Okay, imagine that you're marrying Aarti. Then Neha will appeal to you." Oh, he's straying again. But could he be right? I allow myself to visualise marrying Aarti. **Every single** hair on my body stands to attention.

"I can marry Aarti tomorrow," I mutter reactively. I know my words are bolder than I am right now, but maybe Siddharth needs this intensity to understand how serious I am.

"Dude, you don't even know the girl!" Sid challenges me. I sense a hint of anger in his voice. Or maybe it's irritation. **Panic...** It's panic. I know he means well for me.

"By that logic I barely even know Neha. I really want to get to know Aarti." This is the truest thing I've said so far. I know I mean it. I don't know about the other headline statements I'm boldly making. Can I really marry Aarti tomorrow? Other things being equal, if it were possible, would I? I have goose pimples again.

"*Kya bol raha hai, Nikhil?*" Sid springs up sounding too tense. As if this is his problem to deal with, he starts pacing up and down the room in the aisle between both our beds, making me extremely uncomfortable.

"You know what you're saying right?"

"Honestly, I don't. But, it's true. This is how I feel; maybe I should give it some more time."

"Yes," he agrees too quickly. "Don't do anything stupid in a rush. Think about your families. Your parents, Neha, her parents; they'll all go berserk."

Mental images of all these people with horrified expressions flash through my mind making me cringe and hate myself for thinking this way. Everything seemed so sorted till a few days ago. And now, because of this Aarti.... and suddenly images of her laughing gloriously fill up my mind space, as if to remind me that it is all worth it.

I put myself at instant ease as I assure myself that it's all under control, still a safe secret.

"Ya I'll give it more time," I begin again, more to convince myself than Siddharth. "Hopefully I'll forget all about Aarti once we're back in Mumbai."

Sid gives me another majorly baffled expression. What? What now? Isn't this the right thing to say?

"*Bhai*, what is the problem? Neha? *Ki* Aarti? You don't want to marry Neha because you like Aarti or because you feel you and Neha aren't ideally-suited?"

'Ideally-suited'? First 'berserk' and now 'ideally-suited'? Sid chooses all the wrong opportunities to use good vocabulary. With him, the graver the situation, the heavier the words. I want to let out a laugh like I usually do in a trying situation but now is not the time.

"How does it matter? Either way the bottom line is that if I can feel like this... I mean... If I can have so many doubts at the onset of my relationship with Neha then I shouldn't marry her, right? Wouldn't it be wrong?"

Sid absorbs my words diligently. I rant on.

"Fine. I agree that before I met Aarti... Actually before I saw Aarti, I was quite comfortable with things between Neha and me. But my feelings for Aarti have made me realise that there's nothing special between Neha and me. I've never felt the attraction towards her the way I feel it for Aarti. And it's not even about looks because Neha is really good-looking, probably better looking than Aarti also. It's just... And..... I know, I know this is an arranged marriage and things won't be like they are normally and it'll take time... I just don't want to marry Neha with so many doubts," I finish off.

And with this speech I'm completely exasperated. I just want to close this discussion for now but Sid's keen attention tells me that that's not going to happen soon.

After some thought he says, "Okay, fair enough. But what makes you think that Aarti would be interested in you?"

Ouch! Though Sid says the words flatly without meaning to be condescending and though I'm not wounded by them, they hit my conscience. This is just the reality check I need. Of course! I mean how could I not have thought in this direction? It's not that I think that I'm god's gift to womankind and that any girl I want should automatically want me back. It's just that I've been so absorbed in trying to figure out my own feelings that I've totally ignored a very apparent and obvious aspect in this situation. It's a silly feeling when you realise that you couldn't locate something that was staring you in the face all along.

I give Sid a slight, bouncy nod gesturing him to go on.

"Suppose you can pull off this idea of putting-off this wedding...**somehow**," he says with alarmed eyebrows, "Even then why would Aarti want to be with someone who betrayed her best friend? You know how girls are right....

They can either kill each other or kill **for** each other. Best friends or worst enemies…. She'll hate you bro."

Double ouch. Of course! He's absolutely right! It's as if all my mother's and Ria's favourite Bollywood movies that I have grown up mocking are coming back to haunt me.

Is this really happening? **To me?** I am such a sorted, straightforward, no-nonsense kind of person. I dislike complications, and I'm causing such grave ones at the moment. I literally hate myself right now for having dwelled so much on Aarti at my engagement. I should have just let it pass as a moment of lust, but I knew it was more than that.

And just as Sid's words continue to repeatedly ring in my head I realize something else. It'll never be the same again with Neha now; whether Aarti will ever want me or not. I can't just marry Neha with the notion that Aarti won't accept me after I leave her friend. That's like marrying Neha because I have no choice, and that demeans her essence and presence in my life; definitely not the best foundation for a successful marriage.

I spend the next half hour explaining all of the above to Siddharth, minus the heavy lingo. He accepts my logic with a weak nod.

So I have successfully transferred some of my load onto him, but we still have no conclusion. Not that I expected one, considering the absurd nature of my problem. I feel much better than I deserve to after talking to Sid.

"I think that's for Neha to decide," he says after a few moments of no words.

And I thought we were done!

"Decide what?"

"Whether it's insulting to her or not."

It's my turn to give Sid a confused expression.

He launches into an explanation. "*Dekh.* Whether you admit it or not, you are committed to Neha. You're not cheating on her exactly but I think it's wrong."

"I agree. But I feel it's the right thing to do. It looks wrong now and it's just a bad coincidence that I like her best friend but in the long run it'll be better. Understand this Sid, I have to take Neha's responsibility. It'll be my duty to keep her happy. She deserves a happy marriage. If I don't think I can see her as my wife and more importantly, if I can see someone else in that way, and all this when things have not even started between us, then don't you think it's a clear sign of an unhappy marriage? Isn't it better we face it now than for the rest of our lives?" I sincerely ask him.

I feel I've nailed it this time. Sid has completely understood what I'm saying and he hasn't any counter point. Or so I think.

"I get it, Nikhil. And a few years down the line Neha may even thank you for this when she marries someone else. I know what you're saying but all this is hypothetical. In reality you're here now, to be married to her in just two months. It's easier said than done. How will you even tell anybody all this? Her family? Your family? What explanation will you give? Obviously you can't say anything about Aarti. Nobody will understand that. They'll think you're cheap.

Your bigger motive will go unnoticed... But ya, the wedding will definitely be off. But at what cost? You'll even ruin your image in front of Aarti. And just see what all is at stake. Your parents' reputation. Neha's, most importantly. She'll be shattered...... There's very little chance that this stunt can be pulled off with no collateral damage."

Sid has never sounded this intelligent.

"You're right. So what should I do? *Aise hi shaadi karlu?* How can I just marry her for the heck of it?"

"*Nahi.* Don't do that. *Shaadi ho gayi hoti toh alag baat thi.* But you still have a chance since there is a little time. Are you sure about this?"

"I think so. I don't know about the Aarti part. I'm still figuring that one out. But about Neha I'm sure. I care for her and I don't want to hurt her though doing this will, but, I just can't marry her. Not with so many doubts. It's just wrong"

"*Toh meri baat sun. Pehle toh* give it some time. Think about it properly. *Thode din tak* just see. Maybe you'll change your mind..... If you still want to go ahead and break it off then first *aunty ko confidence mein le.* Calmly make her understand everything and then... you ought to first tell Neha, bro. I don't know if you should say anything about Aarti. She may kill her and then you. But I guess that's justified," Sid manages with sarcasm.

I gaze at him scornfully. Bastard is mocking at my misery!

"Sorry, sorry," he says jokingly "But tell Neha everything as tactfully as possible. I don't know how but it makes sense."

"What reason will I give her?"

"See you can't plan this conversation. You have to go with the flow. Try to do it without bringing up Aarti at all. But if you have to then you should tell her everything. You owe it to her. The whole truth and nothing but the truth," he says poking fun at me. I throw a random pillow in his direction. He laughingly dodges it and continues, "In fact, if Neha still wants to marry you, you should do it."

What?! I stare at him in horror.

"I've got it," he says, like he's got a cure for cancer.

"**What**?" I articulate my confusion.

"I know how you should go about it. You need to put it all in front of her. Tell her how you feel and then tell her that if she still wants to marry you, which she won't want to, then you'll do it for her."

"What? Are you crazy? I **do not** want to marry her."

"I know man, but it's a gamble you'll have to play. This will do the least damage according to me."

"And if she still says yes?"

"She won't. Don't you know anything about girls?"

"Just suppose."

"Then do it, what else? I don't know man! Anyway someday you will marry someone right? This way at least you're not lying to her and she knows what she's in for…. And **trust me** she'll say **no**."

Man! I have underestimated my friend.

"But what about Aarti in this whole situation?"

"Abbey yaar! You're stuck on her only. I don't know Nikhil. It's too complicated. Please understand we're talking in the air."

"Ya, but isn't this manipulating Neha? Purposely putting her in a position like this. Giving the decision into her hands, knowing that she'll say no."

"Bhai, tu kya chahta hai? It's not exactly manipulating. It's giving her the power to decide. I don't think you need to be told how women feel about power in a relationship. In fact this would even improve your non-existent chances with Aarti. It'll make the whole break-up look more mutual."

Whoa! Of course. I didn't know Siddharth was so smart and sly. Right now I could just hug him but I won't. I wish every person was this non-judgemental! I wish people understood that sometimes circumstances are such that we end up hurting someone without actually ever intending to do so. It's inevitable. I know this one deed will give me a tag forever. No matter how good a friend, son, father, human being I am or will be, if I do this, my identity will be subjected to it for a long time to come, if not forever, because you're only as good as your worst deed. Nonetheless, it has to be done. I'm a man of honourable intent and not only do I believe in the one-woman man concept, I have every intention of following it. Sadly, I just don't know which woman!

"Thode din rukjaa. See how things are once we're back in Mumbai. Maybe we're overthinking all of this. Just chill and go with the flow."

Sid's words are now my command. And with this we finally put an end to this endless chapter.

CHAPTER 8

My not-so-brief discussion with Sid comes to a halt and I briefly glance at my watch. It's a little before noon, which means we have less than an hour before we hit the road. The thought of going back home, and getting away from this mess is exciting. But then again, the real mess is in my head. How far can you go from yourself?

Sid and I decide to get ready and pack up. Just before he enters the bathroom, he stalls, and taking a sharp turn asks, "So... Aarti, huh?" with a sly smirk painted across his face. It's as if he just isn't the same person who had a mind-boggling discussion with me on this same subject only minutes ago. This is exactly what his reaction would have been if I'd told him I liked a girl under normal and uncomplicated circumstances. I'm glad that Sid can snap out of a situation so easily.

Embarrassingly I find myself almost blushing, as I try to stifle a smile but fail.

"Hmmmm," I mutter, smirking back.

"*Kabse*? You haven't met her before, have you?"

Oh no. I thought we were done with this subject for a decade or two.

"No ya. I met her at the engagement. Did you **see** her? I don't know what it is man. You know *na* that I would never intentionally want to hurt Neha? But then this Aarti.... I just don't know man."

"It's called 'love at first sight' bro," Siddharth mocks me playfully and rushes into the bathroom before I whack him.

Did he just? Yuck....I feel as if all the cheesiest movies I've ever mocked have ganged up against me to seek revenge.

'Love at first sight.' Is there such a thing? If there ever would be a time when I would subscribe to such a poetic and seemingly unreal theory it would be now. Is this nameless emotion I feel towards Aarti really 'love'? 'Lust' would be more believable to me. But I wouldn't want to ruin someone's life based on just lust for another person. It's too shallow a thing to do.

I start gathering all my scattered belongings meticulously, just like I gather all my scattered thoughts. So finally I've confided my deadliest secret in someone and it didn't go as badly as I'd thought. But this is just Siddharth. I can't expect the same level of acceptance from anyone else.

My phone starts to buzz, distracting me from my packing. Scooping it up from under the pile of clothes, I glance at it. Aarti's number, which I had excitedly saved earlier flashes on the screen. Of course my glee is short-lived as I know it isn't Aarti calling me.

"Hey you! We're all ready. And you guys? Can we come to your room?" Neha asks.

"Hi. Sid has gone for a bath and I still have to go. Just packed. But come *na*. Though we'll be down in 15-20 minutes."

"We're damn bored. Coming down," she hangs up. I quickly tidy my room, hide all my underwear and socks, then gel my hair, put some perfume and sit back to zip up my bags.

"Open *na*," a voice from across the door orders. I do so and Neha, Aarti and Shreya walk in, in ascending height order. "Hi," we all tell each other.

Neha plonks on my bed while the other two occupy the couch placed in front of the bed. Aarti is wearing the shortest shorts I've ever seen on a girl, at least consciously. Her hair still seems wet from a bath. She's wearing an oversized t-shirt that hangs loosely from her torso giving her a tom-boyish look but her girly accessories and lined eyes make her look feminine and Indian. Neha is dressed in a long, pale blue outfit. Her hair seems perfectly in place like it always is. This is the limit to my capacity of noting down girls' appearances so I don't dwell much on Shreya's.

I wonder if Neha had actually figured out which bed was mine or she just sat on it coincidentally. Casual chatting amongst the girls is on and I just smile or nod when something is directed at me. I feel slightly tuned out of their conversation as I try to concentrate on ironing my clothes.

Suddenly the click of the bathroom door gets my attention and I realize I'd completely forgotten about Sid being inside. To his horror and mine, Sid comes out in just his boxers. I mentally kick myself for not informing him about his audience. After all, which guy would want his actual future wife and his fantasy future wife to see his best friend in just his underwear?

Giving me a look that screams 'what-the-fuck-couldn't-you-tell-me', Sid grabs a towel to cover up and after giving the girls a polite smile, he picks up his day's wear and rushes back to the bathroom.

Of all the girls Neha seems the most uncomfortable, and I could be wrong but I think I see Aarti give Shreya a slight nudge as the two stifle a giggle. I realize something is up.

Taking Sid's malfunction of sorts as a cue, Neha winds up the girls' conversation and decides to meet us in the lobby after collecting their luggage. Phew!

By the time Sid comes out again the girls are gone.

"*Abbey saale,* couldn't you tell me?" Sid launches his towel at me.

"Sorry man. Fuck." I laugh and so does Sid. Going by my instinct I decide to enquire…

"Sid, you and Shreya, is something up?"

"Is it that obvious?" Sid asks concerned.

"No, not exactly, but actually ya. She and Aarti were up to something when you went back to the loo."

"Nikhil, you suck! I was in my underwear, man." Sid thumps his forehead with his hand. This is funny.

"Chill. It could have been worse." Thank God our generation doesn't believe in wearing briefs!

"So what's up with you guys?"

"*Yaar,* last night at the bar… you know…" he pauses.

What! This is weird. Men aren't the type to kiss and tell and this, I think is just that, literally.

"When?" I ask, surprised that I didn't notice all this was going on till now.

"Before leaving. Chill, it's not a big deal."

"*Bhai*, you're on a roll! *Tere se toh training leni padegi,* "I tease him, very amused at this development. Sid has never been in a serious relationship. He's a bit commitment-phobic but that has never hampered his streak with the girls.

I wonder what the equation between him and Shreya is at the moment. Almost as if he can read my mind Sid says, "I don't know what to make of it. It was just in the moment. I hope she doesn't think we're dating now.…I like her and all but I haven't thought about dating. We haven't spoken about it since it happened. She avoided eye contact at breakfast also. In fact I was going to tell you to check with Neha about Shreya but you are *toh* stuck somewhere else only. Hopefully she'll talk on the way back."

The way back.…I secretly hope that Aarti will sit behind me so it would mean at least two hours of uninterrupted staring at her face. Maybe I'll get an insight into how I really feel about her. I don't know when I'll see her again. If all goes as per plan, maybe at the wedding. The thought is unwelcome, so pushing it aside I make a quick calculation.

During our stay here, anyone would travel with anyone as per convenience but today the five of us are going back in my car, just as we came. Where Neha would sit in my car is a no-brainer. Out of the other two girls, one will definitely occupy the rear middle seat. Sid will fit better behind Neha than behind me and Shreya will sit next to Sid for reasons now obvious. And this means that once again I will get unlimited access to my new favourite face, full Hindi film style. The thought is juvenile and exciting, and I inwardly give myself a high-five for my detective-like assessment skills.

My phone rings again. We're being summoned. It's time to leave.

CHAPTER 9

I glance at the clock as I get into bed, ready to retire for the day after a rather light and early dinner. It's 9:30pm. This was life 20 years ago on a school night. Why do we ever grow up?

Emotionally and physically exhausted after trying to cope with the events of the last few days, I just need my bed, some solitude and maybe a chilled beer. But, it seems like too much of a task to get out of bed now, so I dismiss the idea. Deciding to call it a night I switch the lights off with big hopes of immediate sleep. Deep down I know it won't happen. My overactive mind won't let go of me so easily. I think it demands at least an hour of pondering and worrying before allowing me to drift into another, hopefully less complicated, parallel universe. Feeling extremely uncomfortable in my mind and consequently in my body I sit up and bury my face in my hands. I know I have to face the facts. I can't escape myself and the best solution for me is to figure things out once and for all. The more I'll think about it, the better I'll know what I want. Reluctantly I start with the facts.

...

So, I've known Neha for roughly two months, if we start calculating from the first contact we had via the internet when I was still in Manchester. I've been working there as a marketing executive for nearly the past four years at an MNC which had hired me after my Masters in Marketing Management from the same city. Professionally I'm at a good point because this firm is compensating me well enough for my slavery, especially if you calculate as an Indian citizen. Despite my average performance in my final year, I landed this job, which till date my parents take pride in showing off about. My mother has been pestering me to settle down, now that I'd run out of excuses – like post-graduation, getting a job, living independently. The truth is that I was also getting a tad too used to a bachelor's lifestyle, and if I didn't think of settling down now I'm not sure I ever would. Organically, over the past one year I'd become less averse to the idea of marriage. Living by yourself abroad can get very lonely after the initial phase. So when my company offered me a better package and position at their Dubai office, I decided to give my mom the green signal. It all fit well. My parents were ecstatic that I'd agreed to start seeing girls and that soon I would be so much closer to home.

Mom always had a few girls in mind, but believe it or not, Neha was the first girl she pitched to me. She had taken it up as a challenge to wed me off before my transfer but I had thought it was a bad idea. It was too soon.

She had confirmed a hundred times that I had no one in mind before calling the Bhatias over for dinner. It was quite hard for everyone to believe that I was going in for an arranged marriage, but frankly, I don't know why! Ria had especially expressed great astonishment. Everyone always presumed that I'd find someone on my own. To be honest, I would have preferred it that way but it didn't happen. It hadn't so far. I'd had my share of affairs and flings, even dated a very hot American who lived in the opposite apartment. My mother was most excited about that one. I think she'd already started thinking about blue-eyed grandchildren, though I don't think my father would have ever approved. Of course, even my mother would prefer an Indian Hindu Punjabi girl over any other, but she'd reached a point where she just wanted me to get married, no matter to whom. My mother would start thinking about the future within seconds of finding out that I had a girlfriend but I couldn't think that far. I guess the general thinking of her generation is that people always date with the intention of marriage. But that was not the case with me. I never thought of any of my girlfriends as prospective wives, let alone mothers of my children. Of course I wasn't even thinking of marriage at those points in my life, and I'd been single for almost two years when I'd agreed to get married. I think I'd made peace with my self-dependence, and the fact that love may never happen to me the way they say it does.

Neha's father, Rajesh uncle and my father had been in the army together before either of them was married. They lost touch after their weddings and moved to different cities. About five years ago they reconnected via Facebook and since both our families were in Mumbai they got well acquainted. Since I haven't been in India in the last 4 years, except for a few holidays, I wasn't a part of their rekindled association. However, my family supposedly knew Neha well, because she was occasionally part of the family dinners and outings. Apparently, she adored my mother and vice versa.

So when my mother told me that she had someone in mind, I knew it either had to be Rajesh uncle's daughter or Priyanka, the daughter of our erstwhile neighbours, the Jaisinghanis.

Mr. and Mrs. Jaisinghani now live in a plush new bungalow on Carter Road, after a massive stroke of luck in the stock market according to my father. Priyanka and I were kids when her family relocated. I'd played with her as a child and though our families are still in touch I've not had any contact with Priyanka since the Jaisinghanis left the building.

My father's first choice was the Bhatias.

During one of their dinners at my place, mom had made an unusual Skype call to me while the Bhatias were still there. So the first meeting I had with Neha's parents was a virtual one. It didn't last more than three minutes and I only saw Neha when she came to say hi for a split second. I was quite embarrassed that my mother was doing this. Of course no one knew why she was doing it; no one except me, that is. I was to return to India after two weeks, and after they left that night, mom told me that she would organise another dinner like this for Neha and me to meet in person.

Siddharth was the first person, actually the only person I told about Neha after my mom said that she was going to suggest the idea of our marriage over dinner with her parents. At that time, the Bhatias had no clue what a dart was coming their way, but my mother has a knack for conveying things to people without actually saying them.

Siddharth had immediately called me after I gave him this news. We generally chatted via messages or the occasional

Skype call but never over the phone. Later, on a subsequent phone call and in a most detective-like manner, he gave me a detailed report about a particular Neha Bhatia after finding her on social media.

Before I actually met her, I knew from my mother that Neha was a 23-year-old, mass-media graduate currently working for a production house in Mumbai. Then, thanks to Sid, I also knew that she had recently gone to Australia and clicked an unnecessary number of pictures there. He also told me that he'd found some rather friendly pictures of hers with some guy who looked a lot older than her, but other than that she seemed like a 'sweet' girl according to him. All of this was information that I could also have obtained if I'd been interested enough to find out. But for some reason I didn't feel the urge to fish out details about her since it was all a distant possibility for me.

...

Sitting sleepless on my bed, I presently wonder who that guy was that Sid had told me about. It's 10:30pm now. I don't know where an entire hour has gone. I get hold of my laptop and fire it up. Some emails related to my transfer await my attention but they can wait until tomorrow, till next week even. I log on to Facebook after a good many days. Ignoring my presumably insignificant notifications I go onto Neha's profile to stalk her. Why haven't I done this before?

Her recent activity says that she's been 'engaged to Nikhil Ahluwalia'. A gazillion 'likes' and 'comments' mark the activity. Ignoring all the overenthusiastic congratulatory comments from friends and relatives and unknown people,

I spend the next thirty minutes digging deeper into her profile. I can spot no pictures of the kind Sid was talking about.

Hmmmmm. Maybe she took them off. Fair enough. Anyway, I have no reason to doubt her credibility. She has been nothing but a good fiancée to me so far.

And then an extremely appealing idea strikes me. I click on the search box and before I know it I'm hurriedly punching alphabets on the keyboard. Alphabets that read A-A-R-T-I C-H-A-T-T-E-R-J-E-E

Wow! There are a significant number of Aarti Chatterjees in the world, but only one significant to me. The thumbnails of the pictures are too small for me to clearly identify **my** Aarti, well in this context, as none of the said girls that prop up has face close-ups in their photographs. I click on the girl that has three mutual friends with me. I wonder who these three people are. Neha is predictably one of them. Number two is Siddharth, the bastard is fast! The third one is some Prashant Bannerjee. Who is this fellow? The name rings a bell.

A minute later I recollect that the said guy is from my school. I haven't met him since we left school. I wonder how he knows Aarti. My best guess is some Bong connection. It's not a big world they say. I click on her display picture and it blows up.

There it is. That sweet, beautiful face I'm obsessed with. She has much more make-up on in the photo than I've seen on her in the last couple of days. She's dressed in heavy traditional clothes and is showing off her *mehendi* to the camera. It's possibly a close family wedding photograph. Aarti is very photogenic, though her live avatar is much better. Automatically, without thinking, I right-click on the picture and save it in a new folder within a folder, then move on to the next picture. It's with some guy. No need to panic. He could be a friend or a relative. Not dwelling much on him I continue to examine her. She seems at ease in the picture, smiling away, held sideways by this tall guy next to her. He seems familiar for some reason. The background of the picture doesn't give much away about its location but it's not India for sure. Hmmmmmm.

I examine the guy. And after two minutes I realise that I know him. I click on the tag. Of course! It's Prashant Bannerjee. What the hell is he doing in her picture number two? I recall how he was in school. He'd had a pretty insignificant existence throughout our schooling years; even more insignificant than mine. We were barely in the same division for a year or two so I don't have too many memories of him.

Then a horrifying thought occurs to me. Something my mind had conveniently never considered. What if Aarti is already seeing someone? In fact, I would be surprised if she isn't. It's so easy to fall in love with her. What if **she** is in love with someone? Or engaged to someone? And what if that someone is HIM? This Prashant fellow! I examine them again. They seem very happy in the picture. Oh no....

My head has really started hurting. Pressing it for momentary relief I realise I'm sweating profusely. I scuffle through the darkness and reach for the AC remote on my bedside and just as I switch it on my door opens slightly and a thin streak of light enters my room.

My mother has come to check on me. She always does this, whenever I'm here.

"*Beta*, why are you still awake? I thought you went to sleep after dinner. Everything okay?" she asks glancing at my laptop, and then says, "Urgent work?" after switching the lights on.

"No. Just not getting sleep," I say shutting the laptop. It's past midnight already. Where has all the time gone? Maybe now my mind will allow me to sleep.

"*Chal*, go to sleep now. We may be going shopping tomorrow."

Oh no. Not more shopping.

"Mummy," I say, almost sounding like a little child.

"*Haan beta*. You need anything? You are sounding strange. Is everything fine?" Mothers are so good with their guess work.

"Come, sit. I wanted to ask you something."

"Tell me?"

I take a deep breath. Do I really want to do this? Can I? And what exactly am I planning to do? I definitely can't tell her anything about Aarti. She'll flip. But I can talk about this wedding at least.

"Mummy, don't you think this is all happening too fast?"

"What is?"

"This. This whole thing," I say making a circular hand motion to go with my words.

"You mean your marriage? Your transfer?"

"Both. But the transfer I can deal with. I still feel we're rushing too much with this wedding. What's the hurry?"

"Nikhil, don't start again. Not now at least. Everything is going so well. Touch wood," she says and jumps to literally touch some wood. Mothers, right? They're too cute.

"Yes, but think from my point of view *na*. I've never met this girl and within 4 months I get married to her. It's **so weird**. I'm sure even Neha is finding it odd. But maybe for our sake they aren't saying anything. Let me settle down over there. I'm at a good position. I'll easily get 3, 4 weeks off again in Jan or Feb. Maybe we can have the wedding then?"

"*Beta*, everything is set. Why are you thinking all this? Neha and her family are as eager as us. They would've told us if they wanted more time. Their *panditji* has only suggested this date….. And you youngsters are so unpredictable. I don't want such a long gap between engagement and marriage."

Oh mom you have no idea how unpredictable we are!

"I know, mom, but at least try and ask them once. The cards aren't printed yet. We can easily still delay it without any problem. It'll be better for everyone. You can shop for my new house also. It's really just a matter of a few months."

"Nikhil!" my mother says shrilly. "*Problem kya hai teri?* Excuses, excuses all the time. I thought we agreed that you were ready for this. How much more will you make me wait! I want to see my grandchildren," she starts her TV-soap dialogues.

No mom! Not the grandchildren drama again. I'm just 29, not 90.

"At your age your father and I were already married for seven years. You were six already," she continues her sob story.

We're majorly deviating and I could really use some sleep, so I decide to let this subject go.

"Forget it, mom. Go to sleep. Forget I said anything."

Accepting this as my withdrawal from the argument she gets up from the bed and comes to ruffle my hair. Then she says, "You both will be very happy. Marriage is a beautiful thing *beta*. Don't be scared."

"I'm not scared, mom. I'm just asking for more time. I'm not saying no. I don't know why this is such a big deal. I have my independent choices. Why are you all pushing me?"

The debate has taken a new turn. My mother gives me a fiery expression and stands still.

"**We** are **pushing** you? **We** don't let you make independent choices?" She's almost screeching. I pray that my father doesn't hear us. She continues.

"This, this whole generation is becoming thankless. We have always let you do what you want, how you want, when you want, without expecting much in return. We want to see you settled. We want to see you happy. Even if we didn't agree with your decisions we accepted them. For what? So that you can tell us we are pushy parents?"

She is absolutely right, and has taken my words in an absolutely wrong context. This is not what I had meant to say.

"I know, mom. Don't get so angry. I didn't mean to say it like that. I know you have always supported me. I'm just talking with regard to this wedding. I really feel two months is a short time to get to know someone, especially to decide to marry them." As I say the words I sound contradictory to my own self. I had barely known Aarti for two days when I'd confidently told Siddharth that I'd marry her.

"**What** do you mean?" demands my mother. "The decision has already been **made**," she tells me sternly.

"Ya of course, but I just don't know Neha. It's so odd."

"Even a lifetime may not be enough *beta*. This is how it happens. For years it's happened like this. You're not the first one and you won't be the last. You know papa and I got married within sixteen days of meeting each other. Are we not a good example for you?"

WHAT? SIXTEEN DAYS? I've grown up listening to stories of how my parents barely knew each other before they got married, but just sixteen days? This meagre number is a revelation.

"**Sixteen days**?" I express my astonishment.

"Yes, don't you know?" she asks, surprised.

"That's too less. Really. It's too less."

"And yet, see how it turned out. You may never feel you know someone enough to marry them. After all, marriage is all about growing together, *beta.*"

Oh god, no philosophy at this hour please!

"Mom, your generation was different. That's why you people married so early also. Things have changed."

"Yes. We were all fools. Only your generation knows how to live. We don't know anything. We're old illiterate people. Do what you like. I am fed up."

"Please, please relax mom. We're only discussing. We'll do what you want. Just calm down."

And just like that, in precisely six seconds my mother's equilibrium changes and she's calm again. Man! Women's moods have unmatched gear-shifting abilities.

"*Beta*, it's late now, why don't you forget all this rubbish and try to sleep? I'm sure you'll think differently in the morning. Why don't you take Neha out for lunch or dinner tomorrow? You keep complaining that you don't know her. It's your fault only. You don't make any effort to meet her… Spend some time with her."

She is one hundred percent right. I've never made plans with Neha. Since I've come down last month she and I have only met for some purpose or the other or when someone else made the plan for us.

"Ya. Maybe I'll meet her tomorrow."

"You are so strange, Nikhil. Any boy in your place would want the opposite of what you want."

"Meaning?"

"Meaning, he would want to have the wedding sooner, not postpone it. Aren't you excited?"

"I am, mom. Goodnight."

"Goodnight," she says letting out an exasperated sigh.

As soon as she leaves the room I close my eyes and slip into an alternate universe immediately.

CHAPTER 10

It's a stunning day today, strangely sunny; sunnier than usual. I'm standing with Siddharth and our friend Amit in a well-mown, lush green lawn, in my heavy Indian attire, waiting for Aarti to arrive. The day I've been waiting for is finally here. My parents, dressed in beautiful, intricately designed clothes usher me to the main stage area and then go to take care of some last minute business. Then our very own version of a priest summons us all at once and we make our way to the *mandap*. I take the spot allotted to me and try to pay attention to what the *pandit* is saying, but my eagerness to see Aarti doesn't let me concentrate.

How beautiful will she look as a bride...**my bride**! I just can't wait. I blindly follow the instructions that the *pandit* is giving me, with no knowledge of the meaning behind the little things that he's making me do. Suddenly everyone starts gasping in awe at someone's entry. I know it's her. **She's here**. I strain my neck to catch a glimpse of her; my eyes desperately searching for her face, but for some reason I can't focus. Everything seems distant, unclear and out of focus. All I can see is a tall Goddess-like figure walking towards me. It's like a spell has been cast on me. Apart from her blurred and beautiful face I can see nothing else.

"Nikhil," a voice calls out to me. It's not Aarti who's calling me and I continue to gape at this celestial appearance walking towards me without responding to the third person.

"Nikhil," the familiar voice grows louder and I feel a tap on my shoulder, shaking me, bringing me back to reality. I wake up with a jolt. Becoming aware of my disappointing reality I open an eye to peek up at my mother who is towering over me, observing me suspiciously almost as if she's got wind of what's in my head.

"Good morning, *beta*. It's 11:30. You still want to sleep more? Papa is also at home today."

My mother herself isn't much of an early bird but 9 am is the maximum time it is okay to sleep till, as per the unspoken but understood rules of our house. Every household has its own mechanism. During my school days, I would wake up as per school time but even on holidays, my father, who is quite a disciplinarian, liked me to be up and about by 9 am. 10 am was his threshold. He never scolded me though. He just preferred things to be a certain way and my mother always ensured they were that way. The two of them have always been in great sync. More often than not, on holidays that my father wasn't at home my mother would let me sleep till whenever I wanted to. It was our little secret.

Of course, none of this matters anymore. I'm not bound by any boundaries now. Papa wouldn't say anything to me even if I were to sleep till the day after tomorrow.

"Send Kunta with my milk *na* please... Actually tell her to put my breakfast on the table. I'll come in ten minutes."

I rush to the bathroom in order to reconnect with my dream. Once I'm by myself again I try to replay the dream in my head. I just can't get hold of her face. I know it's Aarti but I can't see her. And the more I try to recollect my dream the more I seem to forget it. This happened to me even as a child. I don't dream often nowadays. In fact, I don't dream at all; literally I mean. Figuratively I dream big. I have plans of starting my own company and setting up a business in India. But all that is a part of the distant future, if at all. It doesn't fit well in the immediate scheme of things, especially according to my father.

'Now is a bad time.' This has been his standard answer for the past five years every time I've broached the topic of business. Of course he isn't entirely wrong, but part of me knows that he may never favour the idea of quitting a job that pays me so 'handsomely' to start a business of my own. He believes in service.

Over the years, I've seen some great technology abroad that I want to bring to India. India definitely has a good scope and market for it, but 'it's never the right time' or 'the right thing to do' according to my father. He always argues that there are so many better ways to invest the money that we would need for the business; ways which would not only give me a stable bank balance and better returns, but would also keep risk at bay. Who will explain to him that everything is not about making the best choice, but about making the choice that we like best. But I don't push him on this subject just like I didn't push him about the stock market.

My father never encouraged my indulgence in the stock market. In fact, he reprimanded me for it, but I loved it. As a concept I thrived on it. In my final year of college I had got wind of this new world of shares and stocks thanks to Siddharth, who would blurt out all the insightful tips his father would give him. Sid didn't care much for all this, but I took to it very well.

However, my father negated all my trivial triumphs in the market as luck or short-sighted calculation. The truth is that several years ago my uncle had incurred massive losses in the market due to his own poor judgement; so my father is of the opinion that it's a baited-trap. Almost like gambling. He didn't allow me to dwell on it any further than a pastime for some extra pocket money during college.

...

After brunch, I get hold of my phone which I have conveniently disowned for the past fifteen hours or so. I've never been a phone-addict. I recall how Neha has been waking me up the last few days, but I don't miss it. There are two messages from her in my inbox that await my attention. Her phone seems to be working again.

Neha @ 9:40pm – So tired, but had a good time :) will sleep early tonight.

Neha @ 11:06pm – Have you slept already? Good night. Sweet dreams :)

Neha's wish has come true. I did have sweet dreams. The irony is that my sweet dream would certainly be her worst nightmare. Guilt fills my mind again but I shun it away. I have beaten myself up a lot over this subject already. **This** wasn't my fault. One can't decide what to dream of. It just happened to me, much like everything else these days. My mother has a theory about dreams though. She always says that we dream either of things that we think too much about or of things that we consciously avoid thinking about. And I am doing both these with Aarti. So in a way I had it coming. Mom also says that when we meet people after drastic intervals they usually come in our dreams, but that's an irrelevant piece of information.

I realise that I owe Neha a reply or two. Currently, I'm using a make-shift phone until I buy the latest Samsung from Dubai. This phone only has a few games and can't support the umpteen applications that keep people more socially abreast than is necessary. Thank god for that. I don't like the idea of knowing everything about everyone at all times and that's what technology is enabling these days. I am a fan of new age technology, no doubt, but for completely different reasons.

Nikhil @ 12:15pm – Good morning :)

I send her a cursory text message tentatively, and receive a reply instantly.

Neha @12:16pm – Your morning starts at noon I see.

She doesn't add any emoticon to her message making it sound stern and clipped. I can't tell if she's angry that I didn't reply last night or if she's just making casual small talk. Damn text messages for not being able to convey tone! I like texting though. I highly prefer it to verbal phone conversations. Those make me uncomfortable.

Nikhil @ 12:18pm – My time zones are messed up :P

I receive no reply for the next ten minutes so I start my laptop and decide to immerse myself in some paperless 'paperwork' that I need to get going before my transfer.

At 5 pm there is still no reply from her. Based on my decision yesterday to get to know Neha better I decide to ask her out for dinner.

Nikhil @ 5:04pm – I thought we could catch up after ur done with work today.

I text her this and regret it as soon as I've hit the send button. Catch-up? Really? Who says **that** to their future wife? You don't 'catch-up' with your fiancée with whom you've just spent 4 days in a row. Where are the romantic bones when you need them?

I get a reply after five minutes, putting an end to my self-embarrassment.

Neha @ 5:10pm – Hey. Cool. I'll be done by 7. Pick me up?

Nikhil @ 5:11pm – Sure. U decide where. I don't know the best places around here anymore.

Neha @ 5:11pm – Ok let me think. U know where my office is?

Nikhil @ 5:12pm – Yes. Mom showed me ur office building last week.

Neha @ 5:13pm – Ohh. So someone has been stalking me ;)

I'm tongue-tied. Of course I can't tell her that mom had shown me the building because we happened to pass by it and that I hadn't romantically been stalking her nor doing any of the things that frankly, I should have been doing.

Nikhil @ 5:15pm – Haha. See u at 7 :)

CHAPTER 11

I realize I'm too formal with Neha. Maybe that will change tonight. Believe it or not I'm actually looking forward to this dinner. This will be our first proper 'date.' A lot depends on how it goes.

I recall our first encounter alone and try to recollect how I'd felt about it.

...

The Bhatias had come over for dinner to my place and I had just come back from the UK three days ago. It was made to look like a dinner as any other, but every single person present knew of the ulterior motive behind the dinner – to get Neha and me to meet each other. For the most part of that evening, I was cordial but uncomfortable because I didn't know these people well and I knew well what was going on. **It. Was. Awkward.** My mother made Neha sit next to me for everything. If I was at the bar fixing a drink she would send Neha to me to collect it. If I had gone into my room to check on something and took a minute longer than I should have she would send Neha to call me. It was **really** awkward. Mom thought she was being subtle but everyone understood what she was doing. Later, she asked me to go and pick up ice cream from a nearby ice cream parlour, because apparently two dessert varieties weren't enough! I didn't see through her move immediately. I was just relieved to be getting a chance to escape the scene.

My relief was short-lived and replaced by horror when mom asked Neha to join me on this completely unsolicited drive. I just didn't know what I'd do with her. I realized that this was my mastermind mother's game plan to get us talking but if that's what she wanted then couldn't they have allowed us to meet by ourselves somewhere, instead of making a play date out of it? "Neha *beta* you also go with Nikhil to get the ice cream. He'll get bored alone," she had said. She might as well have said, "Hey, you two are probably going to get married and give me grandchildren someday so now would be a good time to say your first sentences to each other in an ice cream shop."

I remember that unnerving drive was very superficial for both of us. For the most part, we only spoke of our literal and irrelevant surroundings like my car, my car seat, the traffic in Mumbai, the humidity because of delayed rains, and unimportant rubbish like that. Before leaving for the drive my mother had taken me to the room for quick, secret and unnecessary tips. She said, "Don't just buy the ice cream and come. You both eat there and don't let her pay for anything. And take the bridge road; it's slightly longer. And don't be in a hurry." It was a silly plot but fair enough. I did everything as per her explicit instructions but to no avail. It was still a mostly quiet and uncomfortable drive. I don't clearly remember exactly what Neha had worn but it was pink and it was traditional. She had looked very sweet. 'Very sweet' was my first assessment of her. She is, no doubt quite good-looking, but the almost magnetic force that pulls me towards Aarti is absent between Neha and me.

At the ice cream shop I'd ordered my favourite roasted almond flavour which she'd never tried before and had liked when she did. She had ordered strawberry. We spoke nothing about our impending marriage, even on our journey back. It was when we reached my parking lot that we finally came to the point. I knew there was a purpose to our meeting and it was not to buy ice cream together. It was to seal the deal. Though our parents had practically agreed to the wedding, in principal, an official 'yes' from the both of us was obviously mandatory. So bravely, albeit nervously I brought it up once I'd parked my car.

"So," I'd said and paused immediately, turning towards her at an angle. She turned towards me with the hint of a smile but said nothing. Her hands were fastened on the ice cream parcel and I knew I didn't have long before it would start to melt. Unable to broach the subject directly, I decided to reach it through other subjects.

"How long have you been working?" I asked her, feigning deep interest in her career.

"With Milestone? Uh… it's been about a year and a half…. I really like it."

"This isn't your first job?"

"No, no. I worked for a talent management firm before this; for a very short while though. It's too cut throat, and the hours were endless…. Of course working in a production house also takes up too many hours but I like the work better."

"Cool. So you must be meeting all these celebrities and big people on a daily basis. No wonder my mother is so fond of you."

She laughed, then said, "Sometimes I do, but not movie stars. We're mainly into TV shows. Our main aim is to better the quality of TV drama in India. Most of it is just crap nowadays. No story, no sense, no performance, but somehow, record-breaking TRPs.... My company is relatively new, just two years old but we have an interesting line-up."

"Ya? Sounds interesting, your work. Although I think my mom is one of those people who love the kind of 'crap' you're talking about. But I do agree that we need some better entertainment here. Actually, I don't know what's going on here nowadays."

We continued talking about our work life for a few more minutes and then I finally found a way to meander the conversation where it needed to go.

"You seem to love your job. You're fine with leaving it? I mean if you move to Dubai... what have you thought about it?"

She shifted in her seat reversing her crossed legs so as to put the leg on top below and vice versa. I realized she was feeling shy and uncomfortable since I had directly said something that implied that we may get married. Also, I think her hands were getting numb over the ice cream.

After a few seconds she said, "I don't know.... I want to settle down. My parents are very eager to get me married though they've never forced me to see boys. They're just very happy with this, umm, arrangement. I don't think they expected it. I mean because you've hardly been here. But I think they kind of hoped for it. I always had an inkling."

"So do you think this is a good idea?"

"Us getting married?" At this point she was braver than me in uttering the words. Once she'd said them I got the confidence to say them as well.

"Yes, us getting married. We don't know each other. I mean, of course, I know it's an arranged marriage, but it's a big decision, especially with you moving to Dubai."

"Do you want this? You've lived abroad for so long. You don't seem okay with this arranged marriage business."

"No no no, that's not what I meant. I just want to make sure that you say yes for yourself, not because your parents think it's a good idea or because our parents are friends."

She gave me a polite smile.

"I could be a serial killer, you know," I joked, trying to make the moment lighter.

"So could I," she humoured me back and winked. We both let out a laugh. I wasn't sure about husband and wife but at that moment I knew that we could be friends. It was a decent way to close an awkward situation.

"Let's head up?"

"Yes. My mother has messaged twice," she informed me.

"Why, she thinks I may kidnap you?" We laughed again.

"No, actually, she doesn't want me to do anything that appears 'too forward'."

I thought saying this to me was 'too forward' but I appreciated Neha's candour.

I gave her a blank expression.

"My mom thinks the girls of this generation are too 'fast,'" she said animating the inverted commas again. I don't know about the girls of this generation, but I wasn't fast enough to make a move on Neha just yet. We'd only just broken the ice.

The Bhatias left soon after dessert that night. Nothing else noteworthy comes to mind about that particular evening, except my mother's conversation with me after they'd all left. She hurried into my room and shut the door behind her, as if we had some major secret business going on. She always does this. We weren't committing a crime but she acted like we were, speaking in hushed, excited tones. She never wants the house help to know what's going on. They are allegedly very inquisitive. And she never wants word about anything to spread before it's a certainty. I've never understood her logic but abide by it anyway. Her dramatic ways are kind of cute.

"How was your date?" she had asked, excited like a child.

"Mom, this was not a date," I protested though it was irrelevant.

"Of course it was, by all means."

"Please. If at all, then you can say it was a blind date. Anyway, it was fine."

"Don't irritate, Nikhil. *Bata na*. Did you hold hands?"

What were we, kids? It's not that adults don't hold hands but it was just the weirdest question she'd ever asked me.

"**MOM**! Please. I want to sleep. Goodnight."

Why my mother would want to know if Neha and I had held hands is a question I'll never know the answer to.

"What sleep? We have to make the decision final. I tell you, we are all very excited. Now we just want a final nod from you and Neha and then we can start the planning. There's so much to do. We all want to have an engagement as soon as possible and then the wedding before you go to…"

"Mom shhhh, calm down," I cut her short. "Why are you in such a hurry? I have agreed to get married *na*. I'm not running away. We'll talk in the morning. *Ab aap so jao.*"

"You leave all that. Just answer me. Yes or no? I know what you will say, so *chalo* now tell me."

"We should meet once again at least. Without all of you around."

"Okay, take her out for dinner tomorrow. I'll arrange it."

"No no, not tomorrow; after a few days maybe."

"*Arre*, why?"

"No, I don't want to take her out."

"So then it's a 'yes'?"

"Okay."

"Okay?"

"As in **yes**. Okay? Now goodnight."

"Don't say it like that. You mean it no? You are happy with this?"

"Yes, mom, yes." I had given her a smile, and holding her shoulders said yes again to reassure her. She was all smiles and tears.

...

I realize in retrospection that I may have said 'yes' to marrying Neha simply because there was no reason to say no. I also realize that presently it's 6:20pm and if I don't leave in the next ten minutes I'll be late to meet the same Neha, who is now my fiancée.

CHAPTER 12

At precisely 6:58pm I pull over right outside Neha's office. It's a six-storey, pale pink structure that doesn't look like it's very old or very new. I don't think the whole building is her office as there are many tell-tale signs of other shops and businesses. The watchman tries to dismiss me without lifting a single limb of his. I make gestures so as to tell him that I'm waiting for someone and will be out of his hair in two minutes.

Within three minutes Neha emerges from the elevator and after exchanging a few pleasantries with passers-by she spots me and flashes a sweet acknowledging smile.

"Hi," she says, as she lets herself in from the passenger side.

"Come, come," I say offering to take her bags and files from her.

She sits, throws her stuff onto the back seat and makes herself comfortable. She's wearing a semi-formal white, half-sleeved shirt and jeans. I don't think formal attire is a pre-requisite in the entertainment industry. I, on my mother's insistence, have worn a crisp white shirt and my best brown chinos. Neha's perfume fills the confines of the car, clearly overpowering mine, maybe because she's just applied it. It's nice, not overtly sweet.

"So where can I take you for dinner?" I'm at my most gentlemanly behaviour. I'm going to give her my complete attention and devotion. I'm not a hopeless romantic so you can't expect me to smell a ladies' perfume and passionately guess which one it is or ask a girl what she's wearing everyday and things like that. But I think I still know how to show a girl a good time.

"What are you in the mood for?" she asks thoughtfully.

"I enjoy all cuisines so any place is fine. Which is your favourite restaurant?"

"I love Italian but my favourite place is all the way in town."

"We can go," I say sportingly though I'd prefer eating somewhere closer.

"No no; too much of an exercise. And that's a very fancy affair. Maybe some other time."

"Okay, then?"

"Ummmm, you know there's this new Mexican joint here, just around the corner. I've been meaning to try it but it's nothing extraordinary. Very small but looks damn interesting."

"That's perfect. I love trying new places, especially the small underdog ones. They usually have the best stuff. In fact, I must have tried every small restaurant in Manchester."

"Me too. In fact, I have a list also. Me, Shreya and Aarti have a deal. Every month we have to try at least two new places. It's a good way to meet regularly also."

'Shreya, Aarti and I' – I want to correct her but obviously don't. Hearing Aarti's name throws me off track, but dutifully I don't let it distract me. It's just a silly, irrelevant mention and I must let it pass. This is going well. I must concentrate on Neha, I inwardly keep reminding myself.

By now the watchman has made the monumental effort of getting up to make his way towards us. Neha gestures to him that we're going away and he seats himself again. I fire-up the car and ask for directions.

"Take a left from the signal," Neha guides me.

The place is literally one left from the curb. Within seven minutes we're entering Café Mexico.

...

At 11 pm I'm in my bed after changing into my night-clothes. I'm feeling hungry again, probably because we had a relatively early dinner, and also because I have an almost insatiable appetite. Deciding to ignore the feeling, I start my laptop to check if my emails from earlier today have gotten any response. Gary, now my ex-boss, is always a bit delayed with responses. He just can't be spontaneous – a perfect excuse to hire Brigitta, a perfectly pretty, model-like brunette. Over the years she's become a good friend of mine. But I have no reply awaiting me despite her existence.

Just as I log onto Facebook, my mother enters the room in her usual ninja-like manner. I'm assuming she's here to conduct an enquiry on my 'date'.

"*Aa gaya, Nikhil,*" she says rubbing her eyes and silencing a yawn.

"No, mom. *Nahi aaya,*" I joke.

"You need to work on your sense of humour *beta*. Surely it has not gone on me."

"Oh please. I'm **hilarious**! **Way** funnier than you."

"Lata *maasi* and Guddu *maasi* will disagree."

"That's because their sense of humour hasn't evolved to my level," I protest petulantly.

My mother has a younger and an older sister. The three of them together are a force to reckon with. They can laugh louder than anyone I know. I have to agree that my mom is a lot of fun, and funny too, but mainly when she's with them. They always have the best time in each other's company. They're very close to each other, not in everyday life, but at heart.

"Okay, okay. How was your date? Where did you take Neha?"

"It was fine. Mom, have you said anything to Neha's parents that may have indicated that I will move back to India soon?"

"No. Not really. Why? What happened?"

"Neha was under the impression that my move to Dubai is just temporary and that in a few years we will come back here."

"Oh that! I just mentioned to them that you wanted to start your business in India."

"**Mom**!" I say in a slightly high-pitched voice.

"What, Nikhil?"

"We can't get into this marriage misleading them about something that is not true. Her parents feel that I will move back. That is not the case. What if I never want to come back?"

"So don't come back. We have not misled anybody. Rajesh and Neelam are fully aware of your transfer and that you are settling down in Dubai for good. But you yourself have shown interest in starting your business here and I just happened to mention it to them casually. Stop finding faults and reasons when everything is going so smoothly," she grouses, utterly frustrated with me.

"I'm not," I only manage meekly.

"Then what is it? Did your dinner not go well?"

"No, it went well.....We went to a Mexican restaurant. It was nice, but not your type."

"Shalini," my father's distant voice calls out.

"*Haanji*, coming," my mother springs up from the bed.

"Nikhil, you are **useless**. No interesting gossip you give me. I was so excited about your date. *Patta nahi kispe gaya hai tu. Chal so ja ab.* Goodnight," she says and leaves after I give her a weak smile and wish her a good night as well. She shuts the door behind her, putting an end to the interrogation and I sit back to analyse my aforementioned date.

...

Dinner tonight was good. Café Mexico is a small joint that will not be able to accommodate more than thirty people at once. The lighting was particularly dingy and gave the whole place a very reddish and bucolic look. It has hypnotic crystal-ball-like lamps hanging atop every table. The lamps were made with chips of stain glass paintings and they made the otherwise dull setting look vibrant. The pricing of the food was not in sync with its apparent small-scale demeanour. We started with some really good quesadillas and followed it up with the usual Mexican fare that is popular in India. Most dishes contained chicken and tasted fine.

Neha's and my choices in food are not very different. She picked three out of the five dishes we ordered and I liked all of them. Overall, dinning in that place was a pleasant experience, and what I liked most was that each and every waiter knew his menu well, and would pronounce the names of the dishes authentically.

Now that the review of the place is done let's analyse my 'date'. If I have to sum it up, I'd say that it was fairly decent. By 7:30 pm Neha and I were already seated at a cosy and secluded table in one of the corners of the eatery. There was just one other table occupied in the restaurant at that point. For most of the two hours that we spent there, we discussed food in various contexts; what to eat here, food in general, different cuisines, favourite dishes, health food, exercising, dieting and stuff like that. Neha seemed determined about fitness. I liked that since I myself am pretty involved in fitness, though I won't give up my vices for it. I like to balance everything.

"I have to put in my papers by the end of the month," she said sipping on her red wine. We were in the middle of a discussion about my transfer and I was enjoying my chilled beer.

"One month notice period is compulsory," she informed me, then added, "I think I'll miss it." A hint of sadness was laced in her voice. And I felt a pinch of guilt. Why do I get to keep my job and she doesn't? Why do I have a choice to live with my parents and she doesn't? Traditions are so one-sided. If we were in love it would be slightly more acceptable, because she would be giving up one thing she loved for another. But that is not the case. I know she's not in love with me; not yet. She's fond of me and maybe now she feels attached to me in a hopeful way, but she's definitely not in love. I think she is really brave to be doing this willingly and happily. Maybe for her parents? Maybe for herself? She does seem keen to settle down.

"I'm sorry," I finally said, acknowledging that I am the reason that she has to leave her job.

"*Arre* no. I didn't mean it like that," she said placing her hand on mine, like we see happening in movies. I felt the urge to withdraw my hand but I didn't. "I don't plan to start working till we're fully settled in. You see, my future husband earns pretty well," she said winking at me.

I realized that Neha was the only one progressing in our relationship. I was stuck somewhere, unnecessarily complicating things. She deserved every bit of reciprocation to her gestures and advances but sheepishly I went on to change the subject.

"I don't earn **that** well also," I said modestly even though I do earn pretty well. "But you'll have to change your field most probably. The entertainment industry in Dubai is quite different I'm sure."

"Ya, that's okay, as long as I get a job. I like working. And besides, if and when you decide to move back here for business I'll think of starting something of my own too. I've always wanted to," she said hopefully.

I was startled by this. I had never mentioned anything about my future plans to her and I think my expression gave me away.

"Or I could join Milestone again. My boss will take me back with open arms. She loves me."

"Neha, I don't know about the business. It's a very distant possibility. I haven't given it much thought even though I want to do it. There's just no guarantee."

"I know, I know. We can't plan so much. I'm really looking forward to Dubai," she assured me reaching for my hand a second time. This time I whole-heartedly grabbed it back. Although I felt none of the electricity between us that I felt towards Aarti, I realized that Neha is a sweetheart and she's willing to adjust a lot for me. She didn't even know me till a few weeks ago. Her eyes lit up at my gesture. This was probably the first advance I have ever made towards her.

Post dinner we went to yet another small eatery for dessert. Neha urged me to let her get the tab at this place, especially because I didn't let her split the bill at dinner. Though I do appreciate a woman who likes to pay for what she eats, I didn't let her. Maybe next time she could treat me. Then we started for her place. This was the highlight of my evening.

While I was driving, Neha invited me to come and watch, as live audience, a reality show that her company was tying-up with on the coming Friday. What is so exciting about this you may wonder… Well, take a guess.

"Come no, it'll be fun."

"I can just come like that? You'll be working there, right? It may look bad."

"Nothing like that. In fact, we get passes to allow people. I'll also be watching it mostly. My work is just for fifteen minutes when my star cast comes to interact with the hosts. It'll all be worked out beforehand."

"I'm not sure. I don't want to pile on."

"Even Shreya and Aarti are coming. It's normal to bring people. Why would I ask otherwise?"

The moment Neha informed me that Aarti would be coming to that event, I knew, I just knew that I would go.

"I can try and get Siddharth in too if you want," Neha offered.

"No, no. That'll be too many people. I'll come," I assured her, feeling involuntarily excited. Aarti was more than enough reason to go. I didn't feel any guilt for feeling excited at the prospect of meeting her. I had given my hundred percent to Neha tonight, and despite having a good time, if at the end of the day I'm still considerably drawn towards another woman then not much is in my hands anymore. How can I bring myself to feel nothing towards Aarti? The more I try to distance myself from her, the more I like her.

Of course, by the end of the night I was pretty fond of Neha; more than I was before. She genuinely is an amazing girl but that's about all I feel towards her. This Chatterjee girl is still all over my mind. And an opportunity to meet her is like an insight into my own feelings.

At 10:32pm on the dot, I pulled over under Neha's building. In India there are no disguised proposals for coffee or tea after dates like in all Hollywood movies. But surely there is some protocol to end a date, isn't there? A hug? A kiss? A smile? I was really unsure about what to do because no move came to me naturally or automatically despite my substantial experience with women. I didn't want to indulge in any couple-like behaviour with Neha apart from the casual stuff. Not until Friday at least, till I see Aarti again, maybe one last time.

Neha and I gave each other a cursory hug and as casually as ever she entered the elevator waving goodbye. I left her building after she messaged me that she was home.

CHAPTER 13

The last couple of days have passed very slowly, in my constant anticipation of the upcoming event tonight. I spent most of my time being utterly useless at home or hitting the gym at our local club. I'm rounding up a little since I've come down because of mom's delicious and loaded food. I think food is a means to express love for my mother, for most mothers. So, if I don't get back to my exercise routine, I can see a paunch on its way.

It's a little past ten in the morning now, and I've just returned home from the health club after a killer workout and swim session. My mother wants me to take her to Crawford market, to buy things that you apparently 'only get in Crawford market'. Usually my mother goes there every few months to stock the house with things that are frankly available everywhere nowadays. I'm her favourite driver and since I'm free I agreed to take her. I have about half an hour before we leave. I quickly type out a message to Siddharth asking him to accompany me on the long drive there. It's a bank holiday and since he has an off he agrees to come along, though I think most other industries are working today. I am to pick him up on the way.

Around 11 am, after a sumptuous brunch made by my mother, she and I leave for the day's work. I have to be back by 5:30 pm in order to meet Neha at Filmcity anytime between 6:30 and 7. This means that my mother has a good two hours to shop and Sid and I have the same amount of time to kill.

...

Once we're in the market and my mother is out of the car, Sid turns to me and says, "So I heard you're meeting these girls tonight?"

Whom had he heard this from? I hadn't mentioned it to him. Wow! This means he and Shreya are still in touch. Are they an item now?

"Ya, I am. I'm sure it'll be an entertaining night," I say wryly.

"Apparently, Neha and Shreya have made a plan to go drinking after the show if it's not too late. Shreya is asking me to come."

Oh! I have no idea about this plan. Neha hasn't mentioned it to me in spite of the frequent texts we've been exchanging. We haven't met since our dinner date on Monday.

And why have only Neha and Shreya made this plan? Isn't Aarti going to come later? Maybe Sid is purposely avoiding her name.

"*Accha?* I had no idea. *Aaja* please. What will I do with them alone?"

"I'm sure you'll have a **blast** with them," he smirks. Bastard.

...

It's fifteen minutes past five when we reach home in the evening. Shopping has been an extremely humid experience today considering that half the month of June has gone by and there has been no rain in the city, just dark clouds, full of promise, hovering threateningly over us.

I'm anxious and excited, mainly to meet Aarti and see how I feel about things now. It's been a few days that I haven't had any contact with her, just aimlessly stalked her on the internet before sleeping at night. I decide to wear my favourite black shirt and faded blue jeans to the do. Within ten minutes I'm out of the house.

At 6:33 pm as per the radio, I reach the main gate of Filmcity. I've heard a lot about this place, mainly from my mother, who tells me that many mainstream movies and TV shows are shot here. I expected it to be a large studio or something, but what I pull over in front of seems like the entrance to a jungle of sorts. I mention to the watchman the event that I am here for and without any further questioning I'm good to go. Inside, I am lost. It's a long and seemingly endless road with grass on both sides, and no sign of any studio in the immediate distance. I call Neha, but she cuts the call probably because she's too busy. I send her a text.

Nikhil @ 6:36pm – Hey I've entered Filmcity. Which way to come?

It's funny I should ask her that because there is only one way ahead.

Neha @ 6:37pm – Sorry I can't answer calls. Keep coming straight till u see a college on ur right. Take the right n then the second left. The studio is right there. Just walk in n sit. Meet u ASAP.

A college? Here?

I do as I'm told and within minutes I'm out of the car and in the studio audience. There are a lot of people here! It's a good thing I won't be noticed. I just want to be out of this place without notifying anyone of my existence. Okay, maybe notifying Aarti. Neither she nor Neha is anywhere in sight. Nor is Shreya for that matter. Not knowing which seats are reserved for us I tentatively take the first empty seat I notice. It's the aisle of the second row from the top and I've just entered from behind it. The place is noisy and abuzz with activity. The performers on stage are in the middle of an ongoing act and the audience is reacting and responding to them on cue. The theme of the act seems to be a political satire, as the protagonist has been rambling on about Indian politics for the past four minutes, which makes sense as it's in sync with the theme of Neha's upcoming show. I contemplate messaging her that I've made it inside and am sitting on seat B15 but decide against it and concentrate ahead.

The stage is too bright and everything too flashy. There are just so many more people and so much more equipment around in the live version of the show than we see when it's telecast. Energetic youngsters, all dressed in black, are continuously running across in the gap between the audience and the stage, communicating on their walkie-talkies. Numerous cameras and camera persons, some even suspended in mid-air sitting on some adjustable equipment, are recording the show. Dancers and stage performers in shiny costumes stand in the far left corner next to the stage. All of this is so well camouflaged when the same thing is aired on TV. My mother would have loved to be here. This is just the sort of thing that she thrives on. Maybe I can ask Neha for a favour and let mom come here next time. I'm going to have to answer so many questions when I get home. Mom was overexcited when I told her about this. I inwardly snort at her silly, cute ways.

After a few minutes I start scanning the area from the left hand side in search of my company, none of whom is here yet. I spot Neha right below the stage, staring intently at it with some papers in her hand. Just at that moment, with uncanny telepathy she looks at me, as if I've called her name or tapped her on the shoulder. Whoa! How'd that happen? I limply wave out to her with an expression that says, "Look, I'm here!" And she returns it with an acknowledging smile. Maybe she had seen me much before I spotted her. She gestures to me as if to say, "I'll be right with you," and scoots over to stand next to a much older and more fancily dressed lady, who I think is her boss. Neha is wearing a formal shirt and jeans. The two of them have an animated conversation which mainly consists of Neha speaking and her boss agreeing or disagreeing with swift nods while her eyes remain fixed on the stage the whole time.

Neha sprints up the aisle after talking to her boss and in a hushed tone says, "Hi," when she's standing next to me.

"Hi," I tell her and think of standing up but before I can she starts to make her way across me further into the row on our right and her thighs fractionally brush against my knee caps.

"Come this way," she directs me as she moves along, softly apologising to the numerous people we have to hurdle across. After twenty seconds of this uncomfortable process I see four unoccupied seats almost at the other end of our row. It would have been so much easier to slip in from the other side had I known the seat numbers. Neha sits down after leaving one seat empty for me, and I end up sitting between her and a very large and very loud aunty. This aunty looks like the type of person who would pat you or give you a high-five after a joke even if she didn't know you. I can imagine her being best friends with my mother. Really, my mother should have been here in my stead.

The two empty seats next to Neha make me wonder again where Aarti and Shreya are. The show seems to be going on since even before I walked in so surely they should have been here by now. Next to the two empty seats are two other very giggly girls. It's been over five minutes since the performers have taken a break and the two are still laughing away gaily. From a bird's eye view our seating arrangement is like this – Left to right: Numerous people-Loud Aunty-Me-Neha-Two Seats That I Wish Were Occupied-Giggly Girl 1-Giggly Girl 2.

Loud Aunty's elbow is nudging into me in spite of the fact that she has claimed even **my** half of the arm-rest. I'm just so out of place here.

"Where are the others?" I somehow muster the courage and ask.

"Shreya's on her way," Neha whispers.

And what about Aarti? I want to ask and I probably would've in a normal circumstance because frankly, it is a normal thing to ask. But because I'm guilty I refrain.

There's a drastic shift in my temperament. Not only am I feeling uncomfortable and out of place, I'm beginning to get irritated as well. There was a purpose of coming here and right now it doesn't seem like it will be served. I sink into my seat and will myself to snap out of my bad mood.

The next gag is humorous, yet predictable. The artists are ridiculing politicians for the massive number of scams they have been responsible for in the last decade. It is absurd that there is so much awareness about corruption in our country and yet such a long way to go till it's eradicated. Momentarily, I'm distracted from my original train of thought and think about our country's future. Then I'm distracted again as Neha's phone jumps to life, vibrating audibly.

"She's here," Neha says to me as she clicks her phone after her brief conversation. Then her attention is back on the stage and I'm side-tracked again.

I hope that by some miracle Aarti is the 'she' who is here but I know Neha meant Shreya. Seconds later I see a girl making her way past Giggly Girls. To my disappointment, but not to my surprise, it is Shreya. She briefly holds Neha in her excited embrace and acknowledges me with a mid-air wave before taking her seat. I return her greeting by mouthing the word 'Hi.' The two start making small talk under their breath and I try my best to eavesdrop. Some predictable excuse of traffic is Shreya's reason for being late. And then they discuss my favourite topic.

"Aarti's not coming," Shreya tells Neha, disappointedly. Fuck. Why?

"Oh!" Neha exclaims.

"She was really going to come," Shreya explains.

"It's okay. Must be stuck at work. I tried calling her sometime back but her phone's off."

"Ya, that's what. Last when I spoke to her she said she has to work late. But she'll try her best to make it. She said she'll call me. Her phone's coming switched off since an hour."

"God knows! I'm sure she'll call when she can. Anyway, watch the show. It's damn good today; better than last time." And then their focus is back on stage.

My mind reels with some emotion I can't instantly place. I think it's close to anger. **How** can she **not** come? This is the closest I've felt to being stood up. She's the reason I'm sitting amongst all these unknown people. I think this is nature's way of teaching me a lesson. I'm finding it hard to think rationally and I'm appalled at how stupid it is for me to be angry because she's not coming. I'm her best friend's fiancé! I really need to get a hold on myself.

Neha's phone buzzes again. "My boss is calling; I think the cast is here. I'll be back in fifteen, twenty minutes," she says and stands up. I wonder if I should move to the empty seat between Shreya and me. Will it be rude if I don't? What is the protocol for this?

"Sit here till I come," Neha instructs Shreya as she leaves, putting me out of my misery. Shreya moves to Neha's seat.

It's odd to be in just her company. I suddenly can't wait to leave. After a little unnecessary small talk I'm completely immersed in the show again.

"Aarti!" Shreya's voice gets all my attention at once. I turn to look at her.

"That's Aarti over there, isn't it?" Shreya asks pointing to a girl who is facing away from us, some ten to twelve rows below us, in the far left corner. In spite of how intensely I feel towards Aarti, I just can't tell if the girl in question is her or not. This girl seems to be looking for something and the more I look at her the more I think that Shreya is right.

"**Aarti**," Shreya alights from her seat slightly and says audibly enough for the girl to hear her, and before anyone can scold us Shreya quickly sits back again.

On cue the girl turns around and the sweet face is indeed that of Aarti's. She spots Shreya and the two wave out to each other excitedly. I'm **ecstatic**. I feel a sudden rush in my body; a rush of adrenaline, or maybe it's excitement. Testosterone. It's probably testosterone. Coming here was a wise decision after all.

Aarti walks up the difference of rows between us and starts to make her way through our row just like Neha and I did. Achingly slowly she inches towards us and I savour the moment as I shamelessly gape at her. Her hair is untied and hangs loosely over her shoulders. I can't tell the colour of her clothes as it's too dark in the audience.

"Hi hi hi," she says to neither of us in particular as she moves past Loud Aunty and starts brushing against my knees. My body tightens against the welcome friction and I actually suppress the urge to catch hold of her. Then all too quickly she's seated next to Shreya making Shreya something we would call *'kebab mein haddi'* in school.

There's such a phenomenal change in my mood that I'm surprised that someone's presence can make such a difference to me. And in that precise moment I know, I just know that I have to put off this wedding.

CHAPTER 14

It doesn't matter whether it is honesty, duty, ethics, moral values or hope, for which I have to put off this wedding, the bottomline is that I **have** to call it off. It would be too unfair to a fine girl like Neha if I were to marry her in spite of what is brewing in my head. And of course, the tiniest hope that Aarti and I are even remotely possible is reason enough to try.

As my mind races with these thoughts I completely zone out all the cacophony around me. I can almost hear my own words in my head. Aarti and Shreya's conversation, Loud Aunty's loudness, the comedian's comedy, nothing is audible enough at the moment. A thunderous roar of applause brings my mind back to the confines of the studio.

When I look on stage, two of yesteryears' biggest superstars are being welcomed with a grand entry. In an attempt to revolutionise the TV industry these two people have come forward and agreed to do this TV show for Neha's company. Everyone is unbelievably excited and smiling away. I, on the other hand, want to throw up. I decide I need to get out from here even if it's just for two minutes. I quickly excuse myself and make my way out to the parking lot.

Outside, I find myself involuntarily reaching into the glove compartment of my car for my emergency stash of cigarettes.

I light one and hate myself for giving in to the temptation. For four months I've successfully managed to keep the habit at bay but I don't care at the moment. The first puff feels strange and causes a slight coughing bout, though the next few drags are heavenly and make me question why I ever gave up this beautiful habit.

I decide that I'll go back inside once I'm finished but when I'm not even half way through, something makes my heart jump. It's Aarti. I see her walking straight towards me, approaching me. I remain as nonchalant as ever about my cigarette but don't dare to smoke in front of her for fear of being judged.

She asks, "You smoke?" Her tone is neither accusatory nor encouraging. It's just a plain simple flat question but I feel at a loss for words. Somehow I manage a weak smile. I think I've lost the art of conversing. Also, I think I'm holding my breath.

"Neha hates smokers, you know," she says playfully, threateningly.

"I don't smoke," I smirk at her and say.

"A smoker **and** a liar? Wow, you're some catch, *haan*," she teases.

"This is a one-time thing. I've quit."

"I'm sure. I guess the show was too stressful for you," she says laughingly.

"Girls are stressful."

"*Arre arre!* Already? This is just the beginning, mister. You have a long way to go."

"I better brace myself for what's coming then."

"Hey! Neha is a darling, okay. You're a lucky guy," she says seriously for the first time.

"I know I know; just joking. Why are you girls so judgemental?"

"Why would you assume that?"

"Smokers aren't necessarily bad people, you know."

"So you're a smoker?"

"No man. And that's not the point." Trust girls to meander their ways out of a subject.

"Okay, smokers are not bad people. Why would you say that?"

"Then what's the big deal even if I do smoke? **Which** I **don't**. Generally, all girls tend to have a problem with it. It's a habit like any other. Neha also drinks."

"You've started a debate. You're in for some trouble, mister. I'm good with debates. Firstly, smoking is very different from drinking. One drinks occasionally but smokes every few hours; generally speaking. If you're an alcoholic, and drink on a daily basis then that's also not healthy. In the same way, if you smoke just on occasions like maybe when you're drinking then that's fine. And Neha's problem with smoking is not because of any moral reasons. It gives her severe headaches. So isn't it justified if she doesn't like people smoking around her?"

"Whoa whoa whoa! Were you into debating in college?" I flatter her.

"Actually, I was," she laughs.

"So tell me, you won't care if your future husband smokes?"

"No, I guess not."

I take the opportunity to prod her further.

"Does your boyfriend smoke?" I ask her, hoping with all my heart that she'll say she doesn't have one.

"Keep guessing," she dodges me. I think I've been so lost in her face, and in trying to survive this conversion that I completely forget to check her out, which is weird because usually it's an involuntary and automatic mechanism. She's wearing a light blue coloured top which frankly is all too sheer in texture and white jeans. A brown bag hangs across her left shoulder and heels of the same brown cover her feet. Her lips look shiny and edible, and she's wearing *kajal*. She's always wearing *kajal*.

"Shit, I think we've been out too long. Let's go back in. They might be looking for us."

"Why did you come out anyway? To spy on me?"

"You wish," she pouts naughtily. "I had to pee actually.... And don't worry, your secret is safe with me," she winks sweetly.

She had to **pee**? Only Aarti can make this unnecessary piece of information sound cute to me.

CHAPTER 15

It's the evening after I met Aarti and I've been pensive and low all day. Along with my feelings for her, my whole agitation with this situation is also increasing by the day. Yesterday was like a stamp on a paper for me. It's given me enough reason to call off this wedding with immediate effect. It just isn't right to mentally betray Neha like this. Cheating isn't just a physical phenomenon.

Of course I know trying to pull this off won't be a joyride! I won't exactly be lauded for my honesty. Nor will anybody concur with my bigger motive, which is to save ourselves from an unhappy marriage. In fact, I'll be severely reprimanded by my own parents if I do this. They'll be furious and embarrassed. And I don't even possess the courage to imagine Neha's reaction or that of her parents'. But despite all this, it's the right thing to do. And all of this won't matter in the years to come. I have to do it even if it means hurting a few innocent people, even if it means losing the slightest chance with Aarti. But what chance do I have now anyway?

I wonder, idly sitting in my room, what it was about her that triggered all this in the first place? Why do I have this incessant need for her, this fatal attraction towards her? I've been through break-ups before, been ditched by girls before and yet with time I managed to let go of people, overcome the feelings. Then why even without any substantial bond am I finding it so difficult to get past Aarti? Somehow, no one I've ever met before has evoked such a sense of longing in me. Maybe there's some truth to the whole forbidden fruit theory, although I'm pretty confident that I would be no less interested in her even if I weren't under the pressure of getting married to her best friend. In fact, if that were the case I'm pretty sure I would be pursuing her. Actually, I'm pretty sure that I would feel exactly this way no matter at what point in my life I met her. Sometimes you just connect with a person for no apparent reason. It could be because of a conversation, a moment, a tragedy, an emotion, a circumstance or anything else. I just can't understand what it is, and yet it's plain and simple, like magnetism.

Despite meeting Aarti just a few days ago I feel like I've know her for years. Despite not knowing anything about her I'm ready to upset my whole life for her. And I can feel all this without an affair, without a friendship even, to be honest.

I've spent the whole day thinking of various ways to pull out of this wedding and yet I have nothing; no concrete ideas. Even the damned internet has no solution for me. For the first time since I've come down I miss being busy with work. I need something to distract me from the constant overdrive my mind is in. Just abandoning this idea and going ahead with things would be so convenient, so easy. But that's the tragedy and maybe the beauty of life, once you know something, you can't 'un-know' it.

I open Aarti's pictures on my laptop. Would I ever not want to know this face? I don't think so. No matter how inconvenient the situation, I could never wish that I hadn't met her.

Is what I feel for her really what they call love? How can it be? How can you love someone you don't even know? What if Aarti is a really bad person, a criminal? I know she isn't, but hypothetically speaking, what if she is?

It wouldn't matter. My attraction to her is not a result of her actions. And besides, humans possess the ability to come to love even the demons of the ones they love, and love them despite those demons.

I repeatedly stare at the same pictures of her over and over again, as if doing that will give me a solution. There's just so much I don't know about her, so much that I want to. An unpleasant thought occurs to me as I study her face. It's the thought of Prashant Bannerjee. Even if **he** isn't seeing her, there could be someone else. And even if there isn't anyone else right now, there will be someday. The jealousy and helplessness I feel is unbearable and stupid. This is all becoming too much. I need an outing....

Sid agrees to meet me at the local clubhouse bar in half an hour. I decide to leave right away in order to just get out of the house and do something. My mother overreacts to the news of my last-minute plan.

"Why can't you inform in advance if you want to go out every day?" she admonishes me.

She tries her best to make me change my mind but tonight I won't cave in. I need to get out desperately.

"Sorry, mom. We **just** made the plan. I don't always inform so late. Only today."

"But I've specially made *bhindi* for you," she uses her ultimate weapon melodramatically, but I'm in no condition to humor her today. Restless as ever to get away I say, "**Mom please**! It's important," in a tone that's harsher than I had intended to use.

"Is everything okay?"

"Ya ya. I'll be home early, don't stay awake. Tell papa I'm taking the big car and don't worry, I'll eat the *bhindi* tomorrow."

I give her a swift hug as a consolation and she sighs. I should really thank her someday for putting up with me. Then I grab the car keys and head for the door.

CHAPTER 16

"What's up, Devdas?" Sid mocks me as he takes a seat opposite me at the bar. I'm just on my first drink so he's obviously wrong. No Devdas in here, buddy!

"*Bol* what'll you have?" I ask, beckoning the waiter.

"Chill out, bro. Let's take it easy."

"*Pakka mat, Sid,*" I brush him off. "*Boss ek repeat mere liye aur ek aur same small,*" I place our order.

Thank heavens for cheap bars. Otherwise what would 'Devdases' like me do? There is low occupancy at the bar today but it's also fairly early. I'm sure it'll fill up soon. There was a time when Sid and I always feared bumping into some family friend or the other at this bar. Earlier the fear was of getting caught drinking, then it was the fear of awkward small talk. Tonight I don't care about anything. I'm in for the kill. It's weirdly exciting, the idea of getting sloshed, just like the good old days, except for my uptight uncle-like company today.

"*Yaar Sid aaj toh peena hi padega. Natak mat kar.*" I need Sid to give me company in this binge-drinking. He cannot make excuses tonight.

"*Haan bhai, theek hai.* I'm drinking *na*, but bro I have a condition." Really now?

"*Bol.*"

"After tonight you're going to put an end to this crap. You'll make a decision, final decision and then stick to it. *Jo bhi ho. Kab kya kaise woh sab dekhlenge.* But seriously this rubbish ends tonight. Cool?"

A minute of silence follows.

"Nikhil?"

"Ya bro, I'm trying..... I think I'm going crazy, Siddharth. What the fuck am I doing? What am I thinking?"

"We'll get to that in a few minutes. Such grave discussions can only be had after three drinks," he says passing me my second drink and taking charge of his own.

Most of our night passes predictably. I drink an inexcusable number of drinks, 8 to be precise, my highest so far. Siddharth plays the double role of getting drunk with me, and curbing my drinking at the same time. He and I have a great time with Mr. Daniels. By the second hour of our meeting I'm pretty tipsy and by the third I'm drunk out of my mind. We remember and reiterate various incidents from our school days and I tell him about Prashant Bannerjee. He's quite surprised at the random connection, though we let the topic pass quickly as I'm not ready to discuss anything in **that** direction yet. Memories soon escalate into future plans, and Sid tells me that he's planning to quit his job in the next three months. We talk about anything and everything two drunken male friends can talk about until we can avoid the topic of Aarti no more. When Sid gathers that I'm not brave enough to bring up the topic, he does.

"Nikhil, are you in love with Aarti?" he asks me flatly. I gulp down my drink in response then tell him that I don't know.

"'I don't know' is not an option. Think of this as a compulsory multiple choice question in an exam and you have to attempt it and the only two options are Yes or No."

"It's not that simple okay."

"Don't fuck the head, Nikhil. Just answer."

I say nothing.

"Okay if the right side was Yes and left side was No, which way would a needle point. What is more likely? Yes or no? And **don't** say middle. I'll really slap you."

He really will. I must say, for the number of drinks we've had, Sid is being quite fancy with all these weird ways to get it out of me. Anyway, a drunken Siddharth is not to be messed with.

"It'll point to the right," I admit.

"So then, there! You have your answer. Problem solved. Cheers."

"But bro, how the fuck does that matter? You don't understand. What will I say to Neha's parents? 'Sorry uncle, aunty but I'm in love with your daughter's best friend so I think I'll just marry her. Okay bye thank you?' Should I say this? No right. And Aarti? Aarti will hate me Siddharth. I'm in deep shit."

"Nikhil, buddy chill. You can't predict what will happen. You're assuming the worst and even if it's true you still can't do something that you know is definitely a mistake."

"What will I say, Siddharth? I can't face my own father. How will I tell hers? It's not possible."

"Do. You. Want. To. Marry. Neha?" Sid says stressing at every word.

"No."

"Exactly!!!! Then don't; not because you think you love Aarti, but because whether Aarti is there or not, you don't want to marry Neha. Just forget about Aarti for the moment."

If only it would happen. I think I'm almost incapable of forgetting Aarti at this point.

"*Chal,* I'll see. Let's leave?"

"*Nahi. Tu kal hi baat kar.* Don't waste more time. You do it yourself tomorrow or I'm coming to your place."

"*Haan haan.* I'll talk tomorrow."

Within the next few minutes we clear the bill and leave. I drunk-drive to my building, another inexcusable thing to do, awkwardly thank Siddharth and then hit the bed as soon as I'm home.

Before falling off to sleep I pray, which is something I haven't done in years. I pray hard that I can endure what's definitely going to happen tomorrow; a terrible, terrible hangover.

CHAPTER 17

"Chal Nikhil. Get up now. *Aur kitna soyega?"* I hear a voice as I come out of deep slumber, but soon drift back into unconsciousness. I don't know how many seconds later but mom says again, "Nikhil, are you listening to me. Are you feeling alright?"

"Hmmm," I hum incoherently.

"What time did you come home last night? I didn't even realise... And what is this; you haven't even changed your clothes! Did you come home drunk last night, Nikhil?"

Wow! That's a lot of words to process. An agitated mother is not the best thing to wake up to when you're hungover.

"No, mom, relax. I'm getting up." When I check my phone I'm surprised to know that it's forty-five minutes past noon.

"I'm not a fool Nikhil. I understand everything. What is the need to overdo things like this? Do everything in limits."

"Okay, I'm sorry. Give me water *na.*"

"Here, take. Have a bath and come to the table for lunch. We have a very busy day. Bhatias are coming for dinner."

Oh no.

Within twenty-seven minutes I'm at the dining table. Throughout my bath I've convinced myself that I have to, at the very least, attempt to broach 'the topic' with my parents before the Bhatias come for dinner tonight. My father isn't home, so now is the perfect opportunity to take my mother into confidence; then it would be easier to deal with my father. This has always been my modus operandi.

Unfortunately, when I'm at the table, all my confidence evaporates into thin air and I find my resolve shaking. I don't even have the courage to lift a spoon. Much of my misery is due to my throbbing head. My mother comes to the table with a swollen and sour countenance and it doesn't take even a moment to notice that she's not in her usual element. This is definitely not the mood she should be in for what I want to tell her.

"Come on, start. What are you waiting for?" she says gesturing towards the *daal* and *bhindi* placed on the table.

"You're not eating?"

She doesn't reply. She just nods, takes her seat and starts with lunch. I forcibly stuff myself with a few bites in order to pop a much-needed painkiller. Throughout the sixteen odd minutes we spend at the dining table mom remains unapproachable, and clearly, my mission to converse with her about my impending marriage fails. I need her to be in her best, most forgiving mood despite which, I know, she will definitely not take it well. And here she is, already hassled. Even she doesn't initiate any conversation throughout lunch, which is very unlike her. As she rises from the chair with our plates in her hands after we are done I somehow summon the courage to say, "Mom I wanted to talk to you about something."

She places the plates back and sits down again, indicating that she's listening. I feel something move in the pit of my stomach. I'm tongue-tied and clueless about what to say. My palms are getting sweaty and I'm just too uncomfortable in my whole body. Maybe we should have this conversation in my room after I've decided exactly what to say.

"Is everything okay, Nikhil? You are behaving very strangely these days. *Kya chal raha hai?*"

"*Kuch nahi mom.* Nothing to worry." Ya, right. "Just wanted to discuss something with you."

"You are scaring me now. Did you drink and drive last night? Are you in trouble? Should I call papa?"

"No, no, no! Shhhh! Stop overreacting. I have not done anything. Is it such a big deal to have a normal conversation?"

"Tell me *beta.* Come to the point."

"We'll talk in my room. Finish your work and come *aaram se.* I'll also finish some email work till then," I lie. I have no work to be done. I'm planning on preparing what I will say till she comes.

With an expression of exhaustion and exasperation my mother sighs. She gets up with a jolt, picks up the plates and mutters her way into the kitchen.

"Fine, let the suspense kill me. I hope you know, Nikhil that your mother is a blood pressure patient. *Pata nahi kya karke baitha hai. Aaj kal bahut ajeeb ho gaya hai tu Nikhil.*" And then she's out of earshot.

My poor mother! I don't mean to add to her woes, but I've got to do this.

All too soon mom is in my room, seated at the edge of the bed, her arms folded.

"*Haan bata ab.* What is the matter? Nikhil, I hope you are not in any kind of trouble. Did you drink and drive last night?

"Okay, mom, forget it. Just forget I said anything, okay?" I try using reverse psychology on her. Let's see if this favourite tool of women can be used on them. "Can't even talk in this house anymore. I said *na* nothing has happened. Still you'll go on and on about the same topic."

"Okay okay, sorry. *Ab tu batayega ki nahi?*"

It's my turn to play pricey. "*Nahi. Aap jaao.* Anyway, you people **just don't** want to understand anything. Forget it."

"Nikhil, please, *beta.* I'm not feeling well. Please tell me, what happened?"

Their species is just too good at it! I have a lot to learn.

"Okay. Firstly, this is **just** an idea, **just** a suggestion, so don't get hyper," I begin.

"I never get hyper."

"Ya sure. So don't now also. Just hear me out calmly and please, please don't overreact."

"Ya ya okay."

This is it. I have to say it. After two long and deep breathes I say, "Mom, I want to postpone this wedding."

This is not what I had wanted to say. I had prepared myself to tell her that I wanted to break this engagement, and yet at the last minute I found myself involuntarily altering my plan of action. Actually, this was Plan B. In case my mother gets hysterical when I tell her that I wanted to call it off, which she would, I had decided that I would suggest postponing for now and then somehow manage to break it off later. At least that would bring things to a standstill for the moment. But when the time came to tell her about my resolve I automatically went with the smaller blow as I couldn't muster the courage to say anything else.

"*Phir wohi baat.* What is the problem, Nikhil? *Tera transfer nahi ho raha kya? Ya koi aur tension hai?*"

"No, it's not that."

"Then why postpone? What is your problem with this wedding? Everything is going so well? *Ek hi baat ki ratt lagaye baitha hai.*"

A long moment of silence ensues.

"Nikhil, for God's sake will you speak clearly? I'm getting tired of these puzzles."

I get up from the bed and start walking up and down the room, surely looking like a maniac. I decide to tell my mother everything, minus the Aarti bit. With sheer courage and no confidence I say, "Mom, I don't want to marry Neha."

A long pause occurs. My mother looks at me as if I've told her I'm pregnant. A pronounced frown forms on her brow and she almost implores me to explain myself further.

"I know I agreed to marry her, and Neha is a **very, very** nice girl but I feel you people are rushing too much with everything. Maybe this is how it's done but I'm not liking it. I'm having second thoughts."

There! I've said it. This is the only brave thing I've done that I'm not proud of.

"**Second thoughts**? Second thoughts about **what**? What is the problem? There has to be a reason. Have you found out something about Neha that you're having second thoughts? She's such a nice girl."

"Yes, she is. And no, there's no problem with her. But I don't want to marry her. She's not the one for me."

"**Why?** Nikhil, don't start this again please. *Kyu pareshaan kar raha hai? Kab tak bhagega shaadi se?* Sometime or the other you have to settle down no...*Yeh sab teri angrezi lifestyle ki galti hai. Tujhe bahar padhne bhejna hi nahi chahiye tha! Yeh sab live-in relationship hamare saath nahi chalega. Ek baar tu shaadi kar toh le fir dekhna.* Neha will keep you very happy."

"Mom, why don't you try to understand? I'm not against marriage, but I don't want to marry Neha. I can't. It's just not fitting. Just because I have agreed to get married it doesn't mean that you marry me off to the first girl you know!"

My mom rises from the bed emitting fury from every inch of her being. I brace myself for melodrama.

"*Hey bhagwan!*" she shrieks the name of the Lord. "What do I do with this boy? For how long will you do this, Nikhil? Aren't you tired? Will I **ever** get to see my grandchildren?"

I think my marriage is most important for the sake of my mother's grandchildren.

"Mom, **please** calm down. I'm just discussing my problem with you. Try to understand what I'm saying... Don't worry; I'll do whatever you want."

Unfortunately, Plan C, which was to pretend to give in and then emotionally blackmail her, also had to be used. It works to the extent that my mother seems immediately at ease when I say this, after all the screeching and hyperventilating. She really does have pressure issues which I don't want to escalate. Of course, I can't afford to lose the momentum so I continue to pursue the topic less fiercely.

"I don't want to marry Neha, mom. Please don't force me," I begin again.

"I'm sorry to say this *beta,* but we have **not** forced you to marry anyone. You yourself agreed to marry Neha after meeting her. You can't just turn away from your decisions when you like.... First you wanted to **postpone** the wedding. Now you don't want a wedding at all. There's always some reason or the other with you. From the beginning you've had problems with commitment. But you are already committed to Neha now.... And you just said that you will do as I say, so as far as my decision is concerned, this conversation is over," she says sternly and turns on her heel to leave my room.

Frankly, I hadn't expected this conversation to go any differently than this, but my mother's easy dismissal and invalidation of this subject infuriates something inside me. I've run out of ways to deal with this and I find myself speaking reactively, unthinkingly.

"**I knew it**! I knew it was a **trap**! I shouldn't have come back only right now! I knew you had this in mind. I should never have agreed only. I don't understand **why** you people are so obsessed with marriage and children! Every person is different and has his own way of life. **So what** if Pammi auntie's son already has two sons? **So what** if *bhaiya* and *bhabhi* have been married for five years. Why should I have to do something because others are doing it? Marriage is **not** the sole purpose of life; nor is having children. And I'm not even **that** old. And let me tell you even if I get married this year I am not having kids anytime soon. So your dreams of having grandchildren will still have to wait anyway!" I finish off, realizing that I've been much harsher than I should have.

I expect her to scream, yell at me, grossly reprimand me but she surprises me with her reaction. The anger and frustration that was emanating from her only seconds ago seems to have subsided. She contorts her face into a grave expression of concern, maybe even sympathy. I don't understand it.

"*Beta*, is there anything else you want to tell me?" she asks in a mellow and mellifluous tone. I have no idea what she has inferred from all that's happened and I'm clueless as to what she expects me to say. I just shrug and nod a 'no' in response.

"Are you **sure,** Nikhil? We will not say anything to you."

What is she talking about?

"Now, why are you speaking in puzzles?"

"Are you gay, Nikhil?" she asks with hesitation etched in her voice. The words are a **shock** to my system. **How on earth has she reached this conclusion**? Especially considering that she's known of at least two of my four former girlfriends. I suppress an urgent need to laugh. Never in my life had I thought that I would be discussing my sexual orientation with anyone, **least** of all **my mother!** I can't bring myself to say anything.

"Answer me, Nikhil. If there is **any** such problem you can tell us. Do you need to see a doctor?"

"Mom, don't be ridiculous. Being gay is **not** a disease and no doctor can do anything about it."

"Of course, I know that, Nikhil. We didn't study abroad like you but we are also educated people. I mean if you have any other problems about your married life you can see a doctor. Nowadays, there is a cure for all medical conditions. Maybe you'll be more comfortable speaking to your father about this?"

No. No. No. Yuck. This is preposterous and weird and way out of line.

"**No mom, no**. You're just being ridiculous now. There is nothing of the sort. Come here. Sit down first."

Teary-eyed and reluctant, she takes her spot again.

"I'm **just fed-up,** Nikhil."

"Okay... I think we should end this discussion for now. We are going off track. Please understand that there is **no** problem of the kind that you are thinking. No big secret. I'm not gay, I'm not a commitment-phobe, and I have no other medical problems. My problem is very simple. When I met Neha I found her sweet. I was willing to see her a few more times and see how it goes because how can you know in just one meeting? But you and papa seemed hell bent on fixing this marriage. I didn't find any faults or problems with her so I said okay. I don't know why you all had to rush with the engagement and everything so much. I had told you that time also that I wanted more time but you didn't listen…. It's not like I've found any problem with her now. But I…. I don't think as a couple we're working. I can't explain it. There's just nothing between us. I want to have something…something **special** with the girl I marry…. All this may not make sense to you, but it's important to me. **Please**. I know this is an arranged marriage and things take time. But you guys are not even giving me that," I say being as clear as I can.

My mother says nothing, simply stares down at no particular thing on the floor with an expression like she's about to cry. She truly is fed-up.

"Now, please stop thinking rubbish like in your TV serials and **relax**. We'll discuss this later. Try to think about everything I've said and I'll also give it another thought. Okay? Don't worry, I'll do what you want," I reassure her, very unsure if I mean it. She still says nothing, even after my masterpiece of a monologue. After a beat or two she lets out a sharp, exasperated sigh and with pronounced steps she leaves my room.

Phew! I lie back on my bed, feeling fractionally better, and summarise this disastrous conversation. What drastic conclusions were reached! At one point I really thought either one of us would have a fit.

After a few seconds, something makes me smile despite the mess I am in. It's the fact that my mother was willing to accept me even if I were gay. I feel proud of her worldly, though inappropriate thinking. Thank god, not all Indians are the same.

CHAPTER 18

To my surprise and relief, dinner last night with the Bhatias got cancelled. I didn't ask my mother for a reason when she reluctantly informed me about the cancellation. When nature does something good for us we shouldn't question it. I think in a way even she was relieved that it was off, considering the bomb I'd thrown on her. After speaking to her, the rest of the day passed normally. We didn't speak much to each other and nothing on '**the**' subject was communicated to my father. At dinner also mom remained as aloof as she was at lunch and I think even my father noticed her despondency. Since I've woken up today she's pointedly staying out of my way and is speaking only when she's spoken to.

Over the weekend, Neha and I have spoken to each other only via text messages, giving each other cursory details about our respective days. She isn't very pushy about meeting up every now and then and I appreciate that about her. As soon as I reach home from the gym I see that she's messaged me asking me to come to her house for dinner tonight.

I had thought that I would rehash the discussion about my wedding with my mother, and subsequently my father in a day or two, and then have the grand finale with Neha after that. But now that she has invited me for dinner I'm in a fix. Declining the invitation will be rude and going to her place for dinner like everything is normal will only prolong this farce, and that's something I don't want to do. This leaves me with just **one** option: everything **must** be done **today**. Anyhow, before I go for dinner to Neha's house I must talk to my father about this. I may not even have to go for dinner if I manage to do this. Tentatively, I accept the invitation.

Nikhil @ 11:42am – Cool. Say around 8pm? and are u sure ur house? We can go out.

Neha @ 11:45am – No no I think moms calling ur parents also. They wanted to discuss invitations and stuff. Our final sample should come today.

Oh no! This is not going to go well. The irony of the situation is not lost on me.

Nikhil @ 11:54am – Oh. Alright see u ☺

I reply and go for a bath.

When I'm out, and seated for lunch Kunta informs me that mom has gone to the gymkhana. Our local club has a lot of activities for members and my mother is actively involved in them. She keeps herself busy throughout the week by attending their seminars and workshops and even involves herself in the social work that they carry out. However, on every holiday of mine when I come down to India, she takes a backseat from such activities in order to devote all her time to me. This is probably the **first** time that she's gone to the gymkhana when I'm at home. I know she's doing this because she's upset with me, and she needs a break.

Actually, the past few days have been stressful for my parents. A long-standing dispute between my family and that of my second cousin's over our ancestral property has not settled in our favour. There is no bad blood between my father and his elder brother but the same cannot be said for him and his cousins. Together my uncle and my father have decided not to be discouraged, and to appeal to a higher court regarding the dispute with my cousin's family. Fortunately, for me and my first cousins, our parents have kept us away from all such issues. Also, my maternal grandmother who lives in Amritsar has not been keeping too well of late. And to add to that I've just made the circumstance more difficult for my mother. It's not that I don't feel bad or guilty about doing this. It's just that I can't afford to waste more time because it's a question of my whole life, and that of Neha's.

...

It's close to three in the afternoon now and I'm still trying to muster the courage to speak to my father about calling this wedding off. Giving bad news to him is always a nerve-wrecking experience, especially deciding how to say it. I recall that **one time,** the one and **only** time I'd failed in a subject in school. It was the sixth grade and the subject was History. I was aghast when I found out, not because it bothered me that I had failed, but because I would have to face my parents. Every day I would go home deciding that somehow, I would tell them that I had failed, but I would fail to do so. Then, on the day of the Open House I had no choice, because I wanted them to know it from me. So I found my mother when she was alone and told her everything. I knew facing her would somehow be easier.

And it was. She expressed concern but dealt with it in a way that was more encouraging than reprimanding. She even did me the favour of conveying this to my father and when she did, I expected him to severely admonish me for my unimpressive feat but he didn't. I still remember he had simply said, "I expect more from you *beta*. Try harder next time and don't let this happen again." He said it with so much disappointment that I think I may have preferred the yelling. At least that way I could hate him and be angry with him for not understanding, but because of his mellow reaction I only ended up hating myself. The guilt was worse because History was his **favourite** subject.

I think that incident did wonders for me. After that I **never** failed any subject and went on to top in History in my final year. Then, no matter what the situation was, whether I needed more money in college, or whether it was my decision to drop science, or whether my parents had caught me smoking, mom always served as a filter, as a shield in these circumstances between my father and me. Not that he would ever do anything drastic, but he was the stricter one out of the two.

Today my mother's absence in the house as I have to break this piece of news to my father has definitely hampered my confidence, but it's a good reminder that I need to start facing the consequences of my actions by taking responsibility for them. It's time to stop using my mother as a messenger for bad news, especially if I intend to keep up my antics.

A part of me still wants to wait till she arrives, lest she accuse me of doing this behind her back, but at 4 pm I realise I'm running out of time. After another half hour passes, I decide to take charge of the matter, and march towards my parents' room with the determination of a nobleman and stealth of a robber; then immediately march right back to mine.

After five minutes, with reinstated confidence I try again and this time manage to open my father's bedroom door which is ajar. He's fast asleep on the bed next to a fat law book and a stack of files. I stare at him for a few minutes and suppress an urge to laugh. My father sleeps in the funniest, most amusing and seemingly uncomfortable position. At any given point while he's asleep one will find him on his stomach, his face on either side, both his legs bent upward, one on each side, his hands wound under his chest. When I was a kid, mom and I would often tease him that he becomes a frog when he sleeps. We'd take funny pictures of him while he slept and share a hearty laugh looking at them later.

It's such a sweet memory... I'm watching my father sleep after an era it seems. I don't know how many minutes pass by as I just stand there staring at him, finding myself unable to wake him up. It feels so wrong to want to wake up a peacefully-sleeping, already hassled, innocent, aging man only to add to his woes and worries.

I will myself to make a move. Now is not the time to be weak. My life is at stake here... He'll rebuke me at first, but eventually, someday, he'll understand. I'll make him understand. I survived the conversation with mom and I'll survive it with him too. I decide to politely wake him up when the creak of the main door of my house breaks my chain of thought. My mother has come home, and within seconds, stands next to me with questioning eyes.

"Kya hua? Ab papa ko bhi pareshaan karne aaya hai?" she whispers.

I'm too shamefaced to answer back and keep my gaze fixed on the floor.

"Nikhil, have you told anything to papa? Is he alright?" she asks and inspects him from afar, then realises that all is well.

Just then, my father stirs up from his siesta and smiles upon seeing us.

"Aaoji. Function kaisa tha?" he asks my mother about the gymkhana event.

"Accha tha. Chai banadu?"

Having the evening tea together is a ritual between my parents. Papa nods a 'yes' gratefully. My mother asks me to help her with something in the kitchen as a way to take me away from there and beckons me to follow her after papa says, *"Beta* Nikhil, get free and come to my room. I have some important things to discuss with you before we meet Rajesh tonight."

Me too, papa. Me too.

CHAPTER 19

When we reach Neha's house for dinner it's 8:32 pm in my watch. This is the third time I'm coming to her place and I'm hoping it's the last.

The Bhatias' residence is a very cosily done up place with many dim lights, lamps, carpets and candles and cushions; too many cushions. Family photographs taken at various foreign locations adorn the whole house. The living area has a very forest-like appeal to it with wooden walls and a faux fireplace. I've always liked it. My house is a more artistic and aesthetic affair.

Six years ago when my father had made a phenomenal sale of one of our rural properties, he gave my mother a lump sum figure to redo our entire house. My mother had put in her best efforts and ideas and she did a fabulous job with the whole place, though everything was more in accordance with her taste than mine and papa's. I wonder how she's still managed to keep everything so well maintained.

The Bhatias prefer to entertain in their guest bedroom rather than living area. They are a family that loves to sing and their karaoke set is the main form of entertainment at all their parties, or so I've heard. The first time I'd come here was a few years ago just to pick up my parents and a few other drunk uncles and aunties who were singing their hearts out. It was comical and entertaining to see them all like that. I don't even remember if I'd met Neha's parents or not but I hadn't met her for sure. The second time was directly before we got engaged.

As we enter their guest room, mom and I sit on two sides of the couch while papa and Rajesh uncle sit by the window so they can smoke. Why does my father get to smoke so openly and I don't? The two of them start discussing something in authentic Punjabi and I engross myself in the match on TV. Mom, Neelam aunty and Neha's younger sister, Jiya, make uninteresting conversation with each other, while Neha is nowhere around. Aunty then organises some finger food for all of us which arrives on a **really cool** trolley tray. **Really** it's just too **cool**, even better than the one my mom has; and I shall be careful never to say this in front of her. The tray has the most delicious looking spread of kebabs I've ever seen and I shall be careful never to say this in front of her either. Maybe I'm finally getting the hang of dealing with women?

I pointedly take none of the appetising appetisers and soon zone out from both the parallel conversations around me. Absentmindedly, mom passes me a plateful of kebabs and with all my will power I nod it away because I'm still angry with her for earlier today, and this is my way of showing it. I know that all hell broke loose for my mother when I didn't eat. It's not a good thing to know people so well that you can take advantage of them. Obviously, since we have company mom can't say anything so, reluctantly, she places the plate back on the trolley. All too soon, aunty is stuffing my face with more kebabs than I can handle.

I've made my point. My mother realizes that I'm still upset with her for forbidding me from speaking to my father about Neha. I was **so** close, literally **so** close. In hindsight I wish she hadn't come home until much later. All along I wanted her to be present when I speak to my father but now I really wish she hadn't come. Whatever his reaction would be, at least he would know everything by now and I wouldn't be here, putting up with this show of normalcy. It could all have been over. If only she hadn't come and stopped me. And that's not even the worst part. She managed this coup with her most melodramatic and filmy move to date; by making me swear upon her life. And what's ridiculous is that it worked. I just couldn't dare to cross her when she used my respect for her as a means to forbid me. What is it about swears?

So now I'm stuck here, in this most horrid and suffocating situation. What does my mother think will happen between today and tomorrow that she thinks I'll change my mind? "Just let it go for today *beta*. We have to go to their house in sometime. We'll discuss this tomorrow. Maybe you'll change your mind after dinner," she had said while making tea for my father.

"Mummy, please let me speak to papa," I pleaded. "How can I pretend everything is okay and act normal when I want to call the wedding off? That's even worse than what I'm doing now. It's intentionally doing something wrong…. We **have to** tell them today. **How** can I do that without telling papa?"

"Nikhil, do you know **what you're saying**? Do you have **any idea** what a big deal this is? *Ek hi baat ki zidd pakad ke rakhi hai jab koi problem hi nahi hai…* Think about Neha *beta.* Imagine what she will go through when you break this engagement. And they are such good friends of papa's."

"So I should let my whole life get ruined? Do something I don't want to do. Does my life have no value?"

"I'm not saying that. Tell us the problem. We'll sit together and solve it. What is the need to break it off?"

"Mom please, we've gone through all this and I've told you I'm sure of my decision."

"Okay, so you have decided *na*. Go ahead then. You are big enough to make your own decisions. Do what you like. Don't speak to me."

I should've known this would happen, and detected the emotional blackmail coming my way.

"Mom, don't be like this. I need your support in this."

"Fine. I'll think about this tomorrow. But for now you will let this go **Nikhil**, for my sake. And you have **my swear, if you respect me even a little** you will not tell papa anything just now," she said and left with the over boiled tea.

I had secretly hoped that papa would've overheard us. That would have been ideal in this not-so-ideal situation, but our voices were too hushed for that to have happened.

So I'm sitting here with no choice but to endure the night in Neha's house with everyone but Neha. I wonder what's keeping her; just then two very bare and very fair legs stand in the spot of the floor that I'm staring at, breaking my reverie.

Neha enters the room, fresh out of a bath in a t-shirt and shorts. She looks nice with her tell-tale wet hair, in this no make-up avatar. She's the type of girl who can look good in any clothes but what I feel towards her is not even the tiniest fraction of what I feel towards Aarti.

Neha greets everyone as she walks in.

"Hi sweetie. Looking very nice. Come sit with us," my mom says to her, then adds, "Nikhil has been waiting for you."

Well-played mom, well-played.

CHAPTER 20

It's been over thirty minutes since Neha has walked into the room where her family is entertaining mine. Casual chit-chat is on amongst everyone as they sip their drinks and enjoy the countless starters that Neelam aunty is serving us. Though my anger towards my mother has considerably subsided, I'm mostly keeping to myself at this dinner and speaking only when I'm spoken to. What may look like shyness to others is really just awkwardness on my part. Neha and I exchange a few cursory glances at each other every few minutes. The few words we exchange are only when she offers me the fresh batches of food that aunty keeps sending from the kitchen. It looks like such a happy picture that I feel a pinch of guilt for wanting to ruin it. I'm really uncomfortable with all these myriad and diverse emotions in my mind.

I'm distracted from my constant thinking when I receive a text message from Neha even though she's sitting right in front of me. My immediate reaction is to look at her, foolishly, but she smartly and nonchalantly continues to talk to my mother, giving nothing away.

Neha @ 9:42pm – This is so odd. Talk na ☺

Nikhil @ 9:43pm – Haha u talk.

Neha @ 9:45pm – Come on. Be a man :P

Nikhil @ 9:46pm – Tch Tch. I don't have to prove anything. Let's see how brave u are.

Neha @ 9:47pm – Are you challenging me?

Nikhil @ 9:48pm – That depends. Do u want to be challenged?

I have no idea where this conversation is going.

I think our relay of messages ends here because she doesn't reply for the next ten minutes. I mentally pat myself for my dodging skills.

Then Neha rises from her chair, collects everyone's plates and says, "Mumma, I'm going to Shreya's to pick up some stuff that I need for tomorrow. I'll be back in fifteen twenty minutes. You put dinner on the table till then. Nikhil, you want to come with me?"

I almost choke on my piece of chicken, even though it's boneless. I'm about to say yes; because obviously I can't say no, when my mother says, "Is that even a question? I'm sure he's been waiting to take you away from us oldies." I just helplessly look from one woman to another.

Okay, I think I'm back to being furious with my mother. But I've got to give this one to Neha though. She is quite smart and gutsy.

As I make my way out of the room I'm relieved to be, well, **out of the room**, but my relief is short-lived as the idea of a romantic drive with Neha at this point is painful and nauseating. I just can't do this anymore. And besides, it's a rather humid weather for a drive, considering the conspicuous absence of rain in June. I'm not a big fan of getting wet in the rain but I hate the summer almost as much as I hate this situation.

As we descend from Neha's house I offer to take my car but she insists on taking me for a drive in hers. We decide to go up till the Sea Link which is a considerable distance for a 'short drive' but it's not as if our parents will complain. I know my mom won't.

CHAPTER 21

Eight minutes into our drive and Neha and I are add of things to talk about. I feel the pressure to make conversation the way I feel it when I meet a guest or distant relative at home. Neha is a good driver and she seems unfazed by the silence between us because honestly, it's normal; but somehow the more it stretches the more deafening it seems to me. While scanning the interiors of her automatic car my attention halts at her iPod. Suddenly I'm filled with curiosity. I've always believed that it's totally okay to judge people based on their taste in music, though over the years I've come to realise that there's no such thing as 'bad music' per se. Owing to the formality that I feel towards Neha, I ask her if I can use her iPod. "Of course," she says to my unnecessary question.

Glad that this will also fill the void in the car that only seems to bother me, I press the aux button on the console and turn up the volume. In a second, the piercing voice of one of my favourite singers fills the car and I'm pleased not only to hear it but also because Neha's iPod houses it. When I check it out, her iPod consists of a diverse mix of music, everything from the cheesy pop songs we grew up listening to, to the latest commercial DJs, from small fry and underdog foreign artists to their Indian counterparts, from mainstream Bollywood to classical Hindustani music. I'm impressed.

"What?" Neha asks me with a shy smile. I hadn't realised that I'm grinning.

"What what?" is the best I can manage.

"What is so amusing in my iPod?"

I laugh a wink. "Nothing. I just didn't figure you for a Tokio Hotel fan," I say truthfully.

She laughs too. "You should have seen me in college. Me Shreya and Aarti. We were crazy fans. We had this whole punk phase and there was a time we would only wear black and all three of us got these funky hairstyles. My mother was traumatised. I don't know how or when we outgrew it."

"You're kidding!"

"No, really," she snickers. Her mention of Aarti makes me flinch but I curb the urge to think in any wayward direction and concentrate on her iPod.

"I'll show you pictures sometime soon," she offers. It excites me only because of the prospect of seeing Aarti's pictures. I smile back in response.

"There's so much we don't know about each other *na*?"

"Ya, that's true."

"And why am I the only one spilling all the beans?" she says with the sweetest expression I've ever seen on her face. I wonder why, all of a sudden, I'm so desperate to detach myself from such a nice girl. Neha and I are compatible in so many ways. But when I think about Aarti it just doesn't matter how perfectly suited for each other Neha and I are.

It doesn't matter that our parents are best of friends and desperately want our union; it doesn't matter that Neha is an amazing girl who would surely make a good wife; it doesn't matter that we have very similar tastes and think alike; it doesn't matter that we're already engaged. It just doesn't matter.

I don't immediately realise that I haven't reacted to Neha as I try to asses things. I feel guilty for putting up an act with her like this. It strikes me like a dart that this is the most opportune time for me to speak to her about things. Fully aware that my parents won't spare me for it, I make a decision.

"Hello? Where are you lost?"

"Neha just pull over on the side *na*."

It's time.

CHAPTER 22

"Here? Why? What happened?" Neha looks at me with a wary expression.

"No no nothing, just pull over anywhere you find parking."

"Why here? Let's go to Carter's?"

"Okay cool," I tell her, relieved that our journey is being cut short.

As she carefully drives on, my mind hunts for ideas to break this to her. I'm not entirely sure if this is the right time to do this but I wonder if there ever will be a right time at all.

"There's this new yogurt place on Carter Road. Let's go there?" she suggests. Neha thinks we're out for a romantic walk in the park but considering what I'm planning to do I have a feeling that the yogurt she's so excited to eat may end up on my face tonight.

"Okay, let's," I say imagining how my face will look dripping with curd.

After six minutes and twenty-four seconds, believe me I've been counting, Neha puts the car engine off and there's pin-drop silence around us as she collects her bag and redoes her hair. I don't know whether I should start talking now or after we're done eating, and then decide on the latter as

Neha deserves to eat in peace. I think Mumbai is currently having a yogurt-revolution. Each time I come down to the city there's a new food fad all over the place with stalls opening up by the dozen. The last time I was down every other shop was selling cupcakes, and the time before it was donuts.

We enter the small shop that cannot possibly accommodate more than five customers at once and Neha places her order.

"What will you have?" she asks me.

"No, I'm not hungry. Thanks." I'm such a bundle of nerves right now that I can't think of eating anything. As if Neha is consciously trying to prolong my wait to leave the shop she leisurely sits and eats her dessert as I look on. I decide to weave my way into the conversation and because I can't bear to wait any longer I start right away.

"So tell me, you've always wanted to have an arranged marriage?" I ask her as casually as possible despite my throbbing heartbeat. She's a bit startled by my question but not in a bad way.

"Umm, honestly, no.... I mean who doesn't dream of falling hopelessly in love and having a crazy romance before marriage?"

I laugh louder than I feel the need to.

"So, then, how come?" I prod her.

"Well, everybody doesn't necessarily find that kind of love, especially one that leads to marriage, right?"

"True."

I don't know what else to say to keep up this conversation, but I have to keep it going.

"But I'm sure you've been in love," I dare to say.

Her eyes shoot up to mine and she tries not to give anything away, but in doing so she actually does.

"So, someone's curious to know about the past *haan*? Good good, that means I get to know your secrets too. **Finally**," she says playfully. I realise that in spite of being engaged we know nothing of each other's pasts. I mean of course, it's not possible to know everything, but surely a couple that intends to marry should know the highlights of one another's past, especially ex-relationships.

I'm slightly side-tracked from our conversation as I think about this.

"I don't know," she says and I have no idea what she's talking about. "How does one know if it's true love that they feel," she says sounding philosophical.

"I don't think you can put a finger on it but there is that something I guess. To be honest I don't know either."

"So you have been in love huh?" she slyly tries to shift the focus on me but I see right through her move.

"I see what you're doing here. I think we were talking about you."

She laughs guiltily. This is good, having a playful conversation like this, like we're friends.

"**Yes**. Yes, I think I've been in love," she says eventually, her voice fading with every word and with a smile that doesn't reach her eyes.

It's nothing less than a revelation when she says it; but of course everyone is bound to have some history. I'm curious about her story so I implore her to go on.

"Whaaaat? I answered you. Enough about me... You tell me, have you been in love?"

Aarti's image comes unbidden to my mind. Really, how does one know if it's true love that they feel?

Neha's eyes are alight with humour and curiosity; and her smile reaches her eyes this time as she anticipates my answer. It makes me realise that we're majorly off track. I shrug ambiguously hoping to dismiss the topic.

"You're a tough nut to crack," she narrows her eyes at me with mock anger. "You've got to tell me **sometime**, I'm sure there's a lot of history I need to catch up on."

As we walk out of the shop and cross the street to reach the promenade I involuntarily start to take deep breathes. We've only walked a few steps on the walking track when I stop in my path and tug at her hand causing her to stop as well.

She looks back at me in surprise and waits for me, expectantly, to say something, but I don't for the next ten seconds or so.

"What? You look like you've seen a ghost," she chuckles.

"Neha....There's no good way to say this," I start off predictably, my heart thumping almost audibly, "So I'm just going to be frank and say it."

"Okay, you're scaring me now. Just so you know I truly hate practical jokes," she warns me.

"I think we're rushing into this wedding."

CHAPTER 23

An incredulous Neha squints so hard at my words that her eyebrows almost form a unibrow. I swallow hard as I try to think of ways to elaborate on what I've said.

"**What?** What did you just say?" she asks in a cautious and confused tone.

I want nothing more than to run away from here right now but my gaze remains fixed on her eyes, which hypnotically command my attention. With some difficulty I find my voice after an extended silence and begin again.

"Don't you think we're rushing into this marriage? We only met a few weeks ago and immediately got engaged, and now this wedding. It's going too fast. I... I don't even know you properly and you don't know me either. I don't know how to explain it. I..." Words fail me.

I'm sweating profusely by now and everything else around us is out of my focus. My full concentration is on Neha's bewildered face, as I try to gauge her reaction and think of sensible things to say. I know I'm hurting her by doing this. She's not in love with me, but it's obvious that she's beginning to love the idea of being with me, which is **exactly** how it should be. Why am I such an ass?

"I don't know where you're going with this and it's making me nervous," she says with none of the obvious signs of nervousness. Her body is poised as ever and her demeanour calm and composed, but her eyes tell me that she's truly horrified. In fact, it looks like **she's** the one who's seen a ghost.

Suddenly I'm thirsty, **just too** thirsty. There's a nagging feeling in my mind that another set of eyes are on me, other than the horrified ones in front of me, I mean. A girl sitting on the bench behind Neha gets my attention probably because we've got hers. I wonder if this is going to be a public spat. I hope not. I've never had one.

Soon the eavesdropper resumes working her phone buttons once she realises that I've noticed her.

"Nikhil, **say something**," Neha demands.

"Let's walk," I suggest. I think it would be a better idea if we moved away.

"No! I need to know what that was about. Are you not happy with things?

"Are you?"

"Of course I am Nikhil. Isn't that why I'm doing this?"

I'm **officially** an asshole.

"Will you **please speak**? What are you trying to say? Be clear."

I'm unbearably uncomfortable in my body and desperately thirsty. I shift from foot-to-foot trying to break eye contact with Neha but keep coming back to her questioning eyes. The emotion she exudes is so compelling and powerful that I find it almost tangible. The **least** I owe her is clarity.

"Can we **please** walk?" I request her and because of the way I say it she knows it's a sincere plea.

Without waiting another beat she darts away in the direction that we've just come from. I hurriedly follow her and in seconds we're briskly marching abreast. Her walk is of a determined and angry person, and when I accost her she mildly pushes me aside and continues to walk purposefully. I stop in my path and have an urgent need to smile. Don't you just hate it when that happens? I always feel the urge to laugh or smile in the most awkward and inappropriate situations.

Actually, Neha's dismissal of me somehow indicates that a barrier is down in our relationship. I feel that often at the start of an association between two people there's a lot of formality and need to please each other. It is when they get closer or spend more time with each other that they are able to represent their true reactions, beliefs and preferences without any inhibitions.

Nonetheless, I'm taken aback when she dodges me and I remain rooted to the spot for a few moments. Neha turns to look at me when she realises I haven't kept up; and automatically, the grin that's painted on my face is wiped off. I hurry up to her and she has the grace to wait.

"Sorry about that. Let's sit on the bench and discuss this," she says. How so nice, Neha?

"Yes, please. I'm sorry."

We walk up to the nearest empty bench and seat ourselves. It's a rustic, light pink, sandstone bench that will surely chafe bare skin, and has the words 'Dedicated to Mr. and Mrs. D'Cunha' inscribed on it.

"You want to postpone the wedding?" Neha asks, directly coming to the point.

I exhale audibly. "I... I don't know. I'm just so confused."

"**Confused about what**?" I'm rendered speechless again. What am I confused about? There's more than one of those things. Truthfully, all the events of the past few days have confused me. Neha, this wedding, Aarti, my feelings, all these aspects are wreaking havoc in my head. Actually it's very simple; I'm torn between my personal desires and my moral obligations.

"**Hello**! I'm talking to you. You're being so strange today."

"I know. I'm so sorry Neha. Can we talk over coffee tomorrow? It's getting late also."

"No, Nikhil. You can't just say things like that and expect me to forget them and agree to come for coffee dates with you. Unless that was a joke, I want to know what's going on."

"Neha, I'm confused about this wedding. I know we're engaged and everything but I don't know…"

My words register a rude shock to Neha but she quickly regains her composure, leans back on the bench and asks, "Are you being pressurised into this wedding?" She's staring me right in the eyes with a look that demands an answer.

"In a way, yes. But not exactly. It's difficult to explain." I sound ridiculous even to myself.

"**Try**," she says with intended sarcasm. **This** I can do.

"Okay, so hear me out calmly."

"Am I not already doing that?"

For someone in the situation she is in, I must admit that Neha has her wits gathered. She has a point here though.

"Yes you are, and believe me, I really appreciate it." It's true.

Still as poised as ever she patiently waits for me to launch into an explanation.

"So I haven't been pressurised into marrying **you** per se. But... uh... you could say that I'm being rushed into marriage, in general... Of course, the ultimate decision to get married was mine but it was more because I wanted to get done with the task. And I didn't expect it all to happen so fast. I feel nagged Neha. From day one I've been telling my parents that I want to take things slow but they seem hell bent on making it all happen before my transfer. I don't blame them and I'm not against marriage, believe me, but I've realised what a big decision it is; not just some task to finish off."

Neha is listening to me with rapt attention, clinging to my every word.

"Am I making any sense to you? I'm so sorry about this."

"Maybe; as in, I'm understanding what you mean. But I still don't know where you're going with this."

I sigh and turn away to catch a breath or two.

"Look Nikhil, I get what you're saying. I've probably experienced it too. I mean I'm just 23, so, there's no real hurry to get married. But I'm looking forward to this new phase even though it's happening earlier than I had thought. I don't know why you're saying all this. What are you trying to get at? Be clear please. I'm sure I can handle it. You want to postpone this wedding?"

Postponing will **have to** do for now. I can't possibly call it off right here, right now; especially after how well she's taking things. I shouldn't be foolish enough to push my luck. Suddenly I feel as light as air, as if a huge physical burden has been taken off me. At least I'm not keeping her in the dark anymore; **not entirely** in the dark anymore. As long as she takes it well, I'll manage the others. It's **her** that I owe an explanation to the most.

"Answer me."

I nod meekly and Neha gets lost in deep thought. I notice two lecherous fellows staring at us, but mainly at Neha. Despite everything that's going on between us I feel protective towards her at this point. I'm actually beginning to get really fond of her. If this were a movie, I'm sure this would be the point where I fall in love with her and then we would go on to live happily ever after; or worse, this would be the point where Neha would turn out to be a really bad person so what I'm doing to her would look justified. But sadly that is not the case, although it would be great for the ease of my own conscience. Neha is testimony to the fact that in life bad things happen even to the best of people for no apparent reason. And I am proof that sometimes even a harmless person with good intentions can end up hurting somebody, even if it's involuntary.

"Let's head back?" I ask Neha as she's still lost in another world. I stand up.

"When?" she asks.

Uh now? "What?"

"When do you want to postpone the wedding to?"

I'm so unprepared to answer such questions but I know I have them coming.

"I don't know." It's my new favourite expression.

"I'm sure you would have **some** idea. Looks like you've thought a **great** deal about all this," she says. I deserve every bit of the sarcasm. She's been nothing but understanding so far.

"Tell me. You can't postpone a wedding **indefinitely; not** after getting engaged and setting a **date, Nikhil.**"

"No, of course not. Not indefinitely," Permanently? I want to add but obviously don't. "Let's discuss all this later please? We should really head back. I just wanted to let you know what was going on in my head; didn't want to keep you in the dark," I say sincerely.

"Why, thank you!"

We start to walk back towards her car with none of the kind of tension that was radiating between us earlier. Ironically, I feel closer to Neha now than I ever have since we got engaged. It's like a friendship has been formed. Opening up to someone kind of opens up the relationship with them as well.

As we wordlessly move towards the parking area I pick up a bottle of water on the way and glug it down.

"Do your parents know?" Neha asks as we reach her car.

"About this?"

'Obviously,' her expression screams.

"I mentioned it to my mother but she overreacted to it. My dad doesn't know. Mom doesn't want me to tell him anything. She feels time will make everything better," I say and immediately regret it.

Neha's eyes shoot up to mine for a second time today. Shit. Have I spoken too much?

"Make **everything better**; as in?"

"You know what I mean," I go for ambiguity, trying to find a way to change the topic. "Want me to drive?"

"Why? Do I not drive well enough for you?" Women get so easily carried away when it comes to their driving skills.

"No no. Not like that. I thought you drove well. I swear." Yuck. Why am I swearing! "I've never driven this car, so I thought..."

"Okay, drive," she says and flings her car keys towards me. We climb into the car and start off.

CHAPTER 24

It's been a few minutes since Neha and I have started back towards her house when she reaches for the car's console and turns the volume down **just** when the phenomenal vocals of an amazing song are about to start. Wisely, I say nothing.

"So where were we?"

What?

"What?"

"Ya, you were saying....What did your mom mean by **'everything will become okay'**? What is **not** okay?"

And I thought I'd wriggled out of this one! "She didn't say **'okay,'** I think she said **'better.'**"

"Same thing."

"It's not the same thing," I protest. I have no idea where I'm going with this. I need to make it back to her house as quickly as possible so this inquisition can stop.

"Okay, fine. Make what **'better'** Nikhil? Stop dodging me," she says with confidence. She's good. I might as well give it up now because I know she won't. I should have just let her drive.

"I told you. I've been having doubts about us," I say very nervously.

"**Us?**" she utters far too audibly. My heart starts to race again. This can go either way. "One second. You said you're thinking about **postponing** this wedding. Now you're saying you're **having doubts** about us. What's happening, Nikhil?"

Why aren't we reaching her bloody building?

"Neha can we **please** discuss this tomorrow?" So that I can have some time to prepare my answers.

"What's the difference? You'll still have to open your mouth and make the effort to talk," she grouses. I'm not offended by the rudeness. I just keep driving.

"Fine, have it your way," she sighs heavily and sinks into her seat; then turns up the volume.

Her skilful anger management does not go unnoticed by me. It's not a quality possessed by many.

As she nonchalantly starts to use her phone I find myself reaching out to the volume dial and silencing the music this time.

"Tell me something; you've never felt that things aren't how they should be between us?" I ask her truthfully. I think my question takes her by surprise.

She stashes her phone away and says, "No not really, I mean I've never thought about it so much. I've never had any reason to doubt anything." "Until now," she adds as an afterthought.

I pull into her garage, careful not to touch the badly parked car next to me.

"Look Nikhil, why don't you clearly speak to me? Telling me things in bits and pieces will not benefit either of us…… You say you don't want to keep me in the dark but by telling me just half the things you're doing that. I know there's more to it than what you're saying. It's so obvious."

I switch off the engine but Neha shows no sign of leaving the car anytime soon. She sits anticipating my answer and the sincerity with which she is conducting herself tugs at my heart. I don't want to discuss all this till tomorrow but she leaves me no choice.

"I just feel 'we' are not working. I mean there's nothing wrong, but something is missing. I couldn't explain it even if I tried."

I have been at the receiving end of such words on so many occasions; I always found such reasons baseless and stupid.

Neha mock-laughs for a nanosecond. "Where is this coming from?"

I shrug.

"Nikhil, this is an arranged marriage. And even though I'm no expert at it I realise that things will take time. Unless and until we make an effort, how will we reach that point in our relationship? Of course, I totally understand that four months is very little time but I think the rush is only so we can time it with your transfer. Because it makes sense. But it doesn't have to be like that."

"Okay," I simply agree because I just want to leave. Not only the situation but even the closed and stuffy atmosphere here, in this parked car, is suffocating me.

"Okay?" her voice echoes. "So what, that's it? Really this is very strange."

"Look, I told you what I felt.... Let's go back now. My mom's just messaged asking where we are. It looks bad," I say imploring her to let this go for tonight.

"Alright fine... Look, I understand postponing. I know this is fast and you may want to settle in on your own before I come. Anyway I think the visas and all will take longer than what we're calculating. So postponing is fine, but..." her voice fades away muting her unasked question.

"But what?"

"By **any** chance do you not want this wedding at all?" she asks cautiously.

Damn! Everything comes to a standstill. I'm flummoxed, just totally thrown off balance by the directness and accuracy of her question. How did she infer this, even if rightly so? Have I made it that obvious? Should I tell her the truth? I don't want to lie to her, but at the same time I can't afford to jeopardise the situation any further than I already have.

Every pore on my body sweats as my mind races with options. I mentally ask myself what I want, one last time, because what I say next will change everything. This is probably my **only** chance to get out of the situation and at the same time my **last** chance to save it as well. I can only take a few seconds to answer her but even eons may not be enough right now. How can I possibly know what the correct decision to make is? One can only decide things on the basis of what one wants and feels. But what if something that is right for me is unfair to someone else? What would I have done if I'd met Aarti when Neha and I were already married? Would I still want to break up with Neha if I'd never met Aarti at all? Sadly I can never know the exact answers to these questions because they're all based on hypothesis.

Going by my gut I say, "Yes."

CHAPTER 25

"What are you saying?" Neha says with rising alarm in her voice. I can literally see her pupils dilate as her eyes widen.

I steel myself and sheepishly look away from her. How does one do this? What should I say now?

The deathly silence that fills our confined space is intolerable.

"You want to break this engagement, Nikhil?"

I'm unable to respond.

"Why? What has happened that you want to do this? I can't believe it. Are you joking?" The shock is evident in her demeanor.

"Look, don't jump to any conclusions. Let's meet for coffee or lunch tomorrow."

"But what's gotten into you suddenly? There has to be some reason…. Or did you never intend to marry me at all? Then why all this? I'm not understanding anything."

I'm not either, to be honest. I rack my brains for the umpteenth time today for an appropriate answer. I contemplate switching the engine back on. I mean if we're going to keep doing this then I need the AC.

My phone jumps to life filling the dark atmosphere with the bright light emanating from the screen. The incessant buzzing sound of the vibration is annoying and I can't ignore my mom any longer.

"Ya mom."

"Nikhil, where are you? We're waiting for you two for dinner. After that you both can go out if you want."

"We're down only; coming up."

"Good," she says and pauses. Then adds, "All okay?"

No.

"Yes."

"Okay, come soon; bye."

"Bye mom."

When I'm done I glance at Neha to gauge her mood. Surely I should be ashamed of myself. She seems to be in deep thought. She's staring intently at something abstract in the air. Her left arm is propped up on the handle bar of the door and she's resting her head on it.

"I'm really sorry, Neha. I don't mean to hurt you," I say predictably.

She doesn't respond. After a beat or two she says, "We should go up."

"Yes, come. Please let's meet tomorrow," I suggest. "And Neha, thank you for being the way you've been today. Really, I mean it." Really, I do.

She nods. She still hasn't snapped out of whatever she's thinking about so attentively.

Just as we both turn outward to exit the car Neha looks at me and says, "Nikhil, does this have anything to do with Gaurav?"

What? Who? Who Gaurav? I have no idea what she is talking about and my expression mirrors my mind.

"Who Gaurav?" I ask curiously. Then something in the back of my mind springs up. Is she talking about that man Sid had seen on her social media profile? My best guess is that Gaurav is an ex-boyfriend. Neha confessed earlier that she's been in love. Maybe it was with this guy.

She realizes that I genuinely don't know whom she's talking about. Reluctant to elaborate further, she says, "Nothing." Then she exits the car, effectively dismissing the subject. I follow suit. As we wordlessly head upstairs in the elevator I wonder how we even got here. We're the same two people who descended this elevator just minutes ago with a totally different equation between us than what we have now. What a difference a few crucial moments can make!

I glance at Neha as we leave the elevator and she looks perturbed to me, but that's because I know she is. A horrible thought occurs to me. What if Neha tells both our families everything that happened tonight? If my mother finds out what I've done she'll eat me alive for dinner over here. I want to ask Neha to keep things a secret for tonight, but I feel too indebted to her already to ask her for anything at all. As Neha rings the doorbell I pass every second with difficulty expecting major drama to follow in the house. The door opens and I almost stop breathing. I feel like such a coward.

As we enter the house, it's like Neha's entire physical existence makes a complete U-turn and everything from her expression to her energy changes radically. She buoyantly and cheerfully meets everyone and conducts herself as if nothing has happened between us or, in fact, the opposite of what actually happened, has happened between us. I'm completely surprised to see her like this and relief courses through my entire body. I rush to the bathroom.

After doing my business I take a look at the mirror in the washroom and give myself a wordless pep talk. Sweat beads constantly mark my forehead like they often do these days and I just stand there for a few moments to be by myself.

"Nikhil," my mother says knocking on the door.

"Coming, coming."

I bet she knows that something is up. In a way it's good if she has an inkling because that way it won't be a complete shock to her when she finds out. When I open the door she inspects me from top to bottom with penetrating eyes and says, "Is everything okay? Are you feeling alright?"

Physically I'm okay, except for the incessant sweating but mentally a tsunami is taking place in my head.

"Yes mom; why haven't you started dinner?"

I hurry out of the room, in a rush to be with everyone as soon as possible, but she doesn't follow and remains fixed outside the bathroom door.

"Nikhil," she calls out when I'm at the threshold of the room. "For **your own sake,** I hope you haven't done anything stupid," she hisses with threatening confidence.

She definitely knows. I don't let her intimidate me this time and stare right back into her eyes. It's my life after all and I have my own way to go about things. I **had to** tell Neha everything tonight. My conscience wouldn't have allowed anything else. Who asked my mother to pack me off on a drive with Neha so happily if she didn't want this!

If I were to take a guess, mom and I have been in this eye-slanging match for about six seconds when Neha audibly emerges from the passage.

"What are you doing here? Come for dinner," she says normally. I take a moment to drink in her casual behavior. I think she's putting up an act of normalcy for the sake of our audience.

She stands slightly away from the threshold of the room so she can't see that my mother is inside.

"I was just waiting for mom to come. She had gone to the loo," I lie.

"Oh, aunty should use my bathroom; not this one," she peeps in.

Mom spontaneously tidies her outfit as if she's just come out of the washroom and looking at Neha she says, "*Arre beta, chalo* start with dinner."

So, the three of us make our way to the dining area for a dinner that I know none of us wants to eat.

Anxiety is indirectly proportionate to appetite.

CHAPTER 26

It's well past midnight when we start towards home from the Bhatias'. The night has gone very normally, considering my unpleasant disclosure to Neha. There wasn't the slightest flinch in her behavior throughout the second innings of our dinner. And I just can't wrap my head around this fact. Either it didn't affect her much or she did a great job of hiding that it did. Frankly, I was expecting a very drastic and dramatic finale to the night.

I'm still sure I've hurt her deeply and I'm not at all proud of what I'm doing. On some level I wanted her to rebuke me, hate me, abuse me even, but her graceful and silent handling of the situation has laden me with guilt all the more. One thing is clear in all this. Neha is not in love with me. I feel good when I reassert this fact to myself.

Even if Neha manages to cope with this situation, it'll be a big blow for her parents because of the weight of social stigma. I wonder how or when this news will be communicated to them just like I wonder what is in store for me when I meet Neha tomorrow. The thought almost makes me shudder. I pray that no one should ever have to face such a situation and I inwardly sympathise with those who do.

Having to stop at a red light at this hour of the night brings my wayward mind back into the confines of the car.

In Mumbai we generally never have to follow the lights post eleven or so in the night, so this is odd. Due to major traffic at a major junction even a constable is present at the scenario maneuvering the restless cars. It seems there has been an accident nearby that's caused this moving trail of automobiles. Luckily no life was lost; a co-driver informs us.

Papa lowers his window and reaches for his cigarettes and lighter, making me jealous of him for the second time this night for the same reason. I wonder why my mother doesn't flout this habit of my father's. I don't think I've ever seen her stopping him or asking him to give it up.

The weather outside is more arid now than ever and it just won't do. The humidity is traumatic for a sweaty human like me. As we reach the first line of the signal traffic I'm glad that dad is doing away with his cigarette.

"*Nikhil, jaldi AC on kar, meri taraf kar*," mom says frantically fanning herself with her *dupatta*.

These days she too has bouts of profuse sweating all of a sudden. It's some hormonal progression I believe.

I take the no-entry to our building because it's a shorter route, and this is something we do only late in the night, though it's wrong at any given hour.

As we step into the elevator of our building I wonder if my mother will grill me about earlier tonight though Neha's behavior has left no reason for anyone to believe that anything could be wrong between us.

Then I wonder if, on the contrary, I should confess to her the actual happenings of the night, but seeing how hassled she looks because of the heat I decide against it.

The three of us soon retire to our rooms wishing each other 'goodnight' although I know that the night neither has been nor will be good for me. After freshening up, when I lie down on my bed I know that sleep will elude me tonight and I'm scared of my own thoughts. This borderline insomnia that I am experiencing these days is really driving me crazy. When I open a work-related email I'm disappointed to know about a professional development. I will be heading one out of the three marketing teams in the Dubai office of my company. That's obviously not the bad news. I knew I would be heading the team before I agreed to the transfer. I'm slightly disheartened at the product allotted to my team today.

On the flip side I know it'll be an interesting challenge for me since it's not what I'm used to promoting, and I will myself to see this change in a good light. After responding to the highly uninteresting email I'm up-to-date with my correspondence. Now what to do?

My phone buzzes startling me slightly. It's a message from Neha.

Neha @ 1:04am – I'm taking a half day tomorrow. Meet me at the Starbucks below my office at 3?

Nikhil @ 1:05am – Sure :)

Neha @ 1:07am – Goodnight.

Nikhil @ 1:07am – Goodnight Neha. Sleep well.

Just like me I know she won't sleep well either.

...

I'm dazed and under-slept and my eyes burn when I wake up. The light of my room is still on as is the laptop beside me. It's pitch dark outside my window so I know it's still in the middle of the night. I don't know at which point while staring at Aarti's photographs did I fall off to sleep. I switch off the light, shut the laptop and close my eyes before sleep can elude me again.

…

"*Beta*, he's still sleeping. Anything urgent?" I faintly hear my mother telling someone on the phone.

I'm quite disoriented.

"Okay I'll do that. Come home for dinner one of these days," she says and I have a feeling that she's talking to Sid.

"Okay. Bye *beta*," she hangs up.

"Who's it mom?" I ask her as soon as she places my phone on the bedside table.

"*Uthgaya Nikhil.* Siddharth had called; for the second time, so I answered. Remember to call him back."

That's odd. I check that it's 10:15 am and that I have no other calls or messages. Why would he be calling for the second time this early on a working day? This cannot be good. I'm eager to call him back but mom is leisurely cleaning my cupboard and it doesn't look like she'll be leaving the room anytime soon.

"Mom, I'm damn hungry," I say hoping this will do the trick.

On cue she swirls as if we're having an earthquake. Okay no, I'm kidding.

"There are *parathas* for breakfast."

"Will it take time?"

"No. Just wait ten minutes. Kunta has just gone down."

"Okay," I say quietly.

After a minute she closes the cupboard and says, "*Accha chal, brush karke table pe aaja. Main deti hoon,*" and then leaves the room to organise my breakfast herself.

Really, it's just wrong to know someone so well. I bolt out of bed, and taking my phone go to my window so I'm out of anyone's earshot. I dial Sid and he picks up on the fourth ring.

"Bro, what's up?"

What's up? He's got me hyperventilating at 10am to ask me **what's up**?

"*Tu bata.* You called?"

"Ya. Is everything okay?"

What's this now?

"Kind of. Why you asking?"

"Dude, look, Shreya called me some time back and said that something is up. She spoke to Neha last night. But she doesn't know any details."

"Oh!"

Damn. The inevitable grapevine has begun its nasty crawl.

"Don't tell me you told Neha everything?"

Why not?

"Not everything, but ya kind of."

"Nothing about Aarti *na*?" he asks with slight panic in his voice. Wasn't Sid advocating that I tell Neha everything?

"No."

"Then?"

"Nothing… just that I want to postpone the wedding for now."

"Oh *accha*. So now?"

"I don't know ya. She's sort of figured everything out."

"How? What has she figured out?"

"Screw all that. I'm meeting her in the afternoon to make things clear."

"What will you say? ….Whatever happens just don't mention Aarti."

Will Sid please stop mentioning Aarti? It's like twisting a knife in my heart.

"Ya I won't.

"Have you thought of what all you'll say?"

"Not yet ya."

"Good luck man," Sid says. I mock-laugh. I really need the luck today.

"*Chal shaamko free hota hoon toh call karta hoon.*"

"Cool. *Ghar aaja. Beer leke aana.* Call me after you're done."

"Cool… bye," he says, but I don't want to hang up. I'm so scared to face Neha today. I'm scared to face the string of people I'll have to face after I face Neha today. Will I even be able to have a beer with Siddharth? Or will the peaceful environment of my house be disrupted after my 'break-up date' with Neha? Will our families be lashing out at each other, spitting out spiteful words? Actually, that's being very optimistic. They'll all just be lashing out at me. My mother will be hysterical. And I'm not brave enough to think about my father's reaction.

"Bro, you there?"

"Sid *yaar,* I'm damn nervous. What the hell am I doing?"

"Nikhil chill *bhai,*" Sid attempts to pacify me. "It'll all be fine. You're doing the right thing," he says with little conviction.

I decide to hang up and put him out of his misery; my misery.

"Thanks. *Chal* bye."

"Bye bro," he hangs up.

This has **got** to be my longest conversation with Siddharth over the phone.

"*Beta,* come to the table. I've called twice," mom says entering my room when I'm typing out a message to Neha.

Nikhil @ 10:39am – See you at 3 :)

…

Three and a half hours later my mother comes to my room to call me to the dining table for lunch.

"*Chal aaja, khaana kha le.*"

Thanks to my meeting with Neha being just a few minutes away, I can't possibly think of eating right now. I just want to be done with today.

"Keep it in the oven *na*. I'll have it later," I tell her, pretending to be busy on my laptop, hoping to dismiss the topic and my mother. She doesn't seem pleased and scolds me for my erratic eating habits these days.

"*Yeh hi hoga na. Gyara gyara baje tak nashta nahi karoge toh bhookh kaha se lagegi lunch keliye. Le lena baad mein. Aur raita fridge main hai.*"

Within ten minutes I'm ready and out of the house.

CHAPTER 27

When I type out a message to Neha informing her that I've reached the coffee shop it's 3:03pm. She replies instantly, telling me that she's crossing over to the place. The atmosphere of the coffee shop is busy and upbeat. I wonder how I'll go about my task in the company of so many strangers. It's not possible to plan such a conversation. I have a vague idea of what to say but I've mainly decided to go with the flow, sincerely hoping that I don't get a steaming cup of coffee on my face at any point of our meeting.

I take up a table setting for two at the far end of the coffee shop, alongside a floor-to-ceiling glass window. Beyond it is a grey stone wall. Maybe I should take another table, closer to the door. What if I have to run?

I love mentally humouring myself in tense situations. It's such a welcome distraction.

Neha walks in a minute or two after I've taken a seat. She takes a good look around before finally spotting me. There's a reluctant and supressed smile on her face as she acknowledges me. She's dressed in a sharp black half-sleeved shirt that digs into the middle of her waist and then flairs out. Her jeans cling to her legs as if for life and she appears lean and lanky in her heels. As she takes a seat opposite me I note that she's looking good, except for her eyes, which aren't bright like they always are and she seems bothered, which I know she is.

"Hi," she says almost remorsefully, with a smile on her face.

"Hi, Neha, thank you for taking a half day to meet me."

She sighs and nods animatedly, conveying that it was a big deal and a hectic day at work.

"Busy day?"

"Ya, pretty hectic," she says and turns slightly to look at the blackboard menu hoisted above the billing counter of the shop. Since the place has self-service we'll have to go and place our orders before we begin 'the talk'.

"Let's go order," she suggests.

"Come."

I queue up behind the three or four people ready to order ahead of us and Neha stands beside me considering her choices. As we move ahead I graze through the menu board but despite skipping lunch I don't have the nerve to eat or drink at the moment.

"What'll you have?" I ask her as we reach the counter.

"I want the white chocolate mocha, your smallest size," she directs the guy at the counter.

"Yes ma'am; your name?" She spells it out.

I'm not really a coffee person so I order a small regular hot chocolate. I insist on getting the tab for our drinks and after some mild jostling Neha lets me. The fellow taking our order grins knowingly. He's definitely used to this sight. He must be thinking we're such a cute couple, on a date in a coffee shop, fighting over the bill. Little does he know…!

As we walk back to our table the atmosphere between us is light and formal but as we take our seats I know this vibe will change soon.

After a few minutes of trivial talk Neha says, "So let's cut to the chase," staring me right in the eyes. I feel my cheeks heat up, swallow hard and damn myself for not thinking this through. I didn't even have the spine to bring it up. It may look like I'm a selfish little indecisive bastard, but really I'm not. I'll truly hate myself for being the reason that Neha has to go through this and that's the reason I can't do this so easily. But the truth is that, like most of us, my needs and wants are the most important to me.

"Say something," Neha admonishes my silence and I get the horrible feeling that this is going to be a repeat telecast of last night.

"Neha, I don't know what to say or how to do this," I go for honesty.

She laughs sarcastically.

"Haven't ever dumped someone before?"

I feel the urge to laugh but then it changes to a bittersweet emotion that leaves a sour taste in my mouth. If only two people could really go through a tough situation with humour.

"No, I haven't ever dumped anyone before." I have actually. Once.

"There's a first time for everything. Go right ahead," she says resigned in her seat.

"White chocolate mocha for Neha," a loud voice summons us.

I collect both our beverages and come to the table. After I hand over Neha's drink to her and take my seat something changes in my mind. No, don't worry; I don't suddenly fall in love with her. I told you this is **not** a movie.

Something I can't put a finger on instils confidence in me and gives my resolve a new lease of life. As Neha wordlessly sips on her drink I go through a pounding of emotions. I have **never** purposely wanted to hurt this girl and everything that's happened has happened naturally. Must I feel so guilty for being attracted to someone or for trying to be honest in my endeavours? Should I not give her, at the very least, a decent break-up without her having to fish out the details? Of course I can't just tell her, 'Hey, you know what, I know we're engaged and all that but I don't think we should marry because I have no feelings for you other than that of friendship and also because I'm in love with your best friend.'

But I've decided to call this wedding off irrespective of a third person's involvement, because on our own the two of us haven't hit it off and that's a shortcoming on neither of our parts. Sometimes a combination just doesn't work in spite of what it's made of. Even if I could manage to feel towards Neha half the emotions that I feel towards Aarti I would not be doing this right now. But once you know how good it can get, why will you want to settle for anything less than that? Aarti has shown me the height and depth that my feelings are capable of reaching and I'm ready to marry any woman who can make me feel the way she does. Obviously, I can convey none of this to Neha but I must at least be comforting in my words to her because she has been so gracious and easy-to-deal-with in our short association with each other.

"Neha," I begin with purpose. "Please don't say it like how you were."

"Say what?" she says placing her mug down and leaning forward.

"That I'm dumping you."

"But isn't that what you're doing?"

"Why debase yourself on my account? You know what you are worth and so do I. You're deserving in every way."

"Your actions don't match your words," she counters fairly.

"Neha, who am **I** to **dump** you? It's a very harsh thing to say and I prefer you don't ever think of this in that way."

"Okay, since everything is about your preferences anyway." Man, she's sharp.

After a few seconds, I try again.

"I'm really sorry. None of this is your fault. Nothing that you have done has caused this and I genuinely am sorry."

"Oh please, Nikhil," Neha feigns laughter. "Don't tell me you're giving me the 'It's not you, it's me' bullshit."

"It's not you or me, Neha. It's **us**." I don't know from where the inspiration to say this has hit me but I'm glad it has. I now have Neha's full attention and curiosity.

"What do you mean?" she says squinting at me.

"Neha, look at us. Apart from yesterday, consider all the time since we've met. Don't you think something is missing between us?"

Isn't this usually the girl's line? Men as a species should just disown me.

"Maybe, but I'm feeling this only because you've put it in my head since last night. I told you I never expected us to be like Romeo and Juliet. Arranged marriages are like this only. I've seen it with so many people. Things change with time you know."

"Sure, things can change at any time, but shouldn't this be the best part; the best phase?"

"It should be the most exciting part, yes, I agree, but it doesn't have to be the same for everyone. I really thought that it'll be all those things that it isn't once we get married and move to Dubai and start living with each other. I never doubted that we'll also be like those crazy couples in love. It would happen someday if not now."

"But there's no guarantee, Neha. I know we're not incompatible, we have similar backgrounds, and most of the things fit. But just because there is no reason not to marry each other, does it mean we should marry?"

"No, not compulsorily. But isn't that how arranged marriages work, Nikhil? I mean you didn't find me on the road and check if there were no reasons not to marry me. I'm sure even you know that this is how it happens. We're not the first two people who've met through their parents for an arranged marriage. You're the first guy my parents suggested and I didn't mind it in the beginning, then slowly I started liking the idea and my parents were only too happy, so we said yes. It was that simple. And I'm sure that's how it happened with you too. Then, suddenly, I don't know what changed," she says and catches her breath; then continues, "Look, Nikhil, I can't force you to do something you don't want to do. I don't feel I have that right over you to ask you to try, but you say things aren't good, or could be better, but honestly how long has it been? How can you judge so fast?"

I quietly assimilate her words and logic.

"Tell me. I just can't understand your decision."

Neha is so calm and collected, it's disarming. At this point we're like two educated people, maybe lawyers, negotiating and reasoning with each other, each asking for their rights and a logical explanation to the other's opinions. I don't know if my feelings about things are coming across to Neha as they are but because of the way our meeting is going I'm feeling relaxed and at ease. If she takes things at this rate then I can nurse the hope that our families will go through this storm in a mature and dignified manner.

"Fine, don't answer me. Have your drink at least. You might as well have ordered cold chocolate."

Ugh. My 'hot' chocolate is anything but. It's not appetizing at all. On second thoughts, I can manage a sip or two. In fact I suddenly really need to have something. The hollowness in my stomach is too apparent to me at the moment. I have some of my drink and instantly feel good. It seems like I won't need that Eno in my pocket after all.

I realise it's my turn to talk, offer an explanation.

"See, everything you've said makes absolute sense and I agree with it Neha. I'm aware how an arranged marriage is and yes, I take full responsibility for saying yes to this marriage. But in the last few days I haven't felt comfortable or sure about this decision. Rightly or wrongly I've been having so many doubts. You tell me, what should I do? Should I ignore everything and blindly go along with things? And what if after marriage we realise that it's not working? Isn't it better we go through this now?"

"But why are you assuming that things will go wrong? Even if we're not running around trees singing songs with each other it's not like we're fighting everyday right? Nothing has gone wrong till now. Or has it? Actually, I'm sure something has happened and you're not telling me. But you should. I'm sure I'll have an explanation for any questions that you have. Tell me honestly."

"Believe me, Neha, nothing has happened."

She lets out an exasperated sigh and sinks back into her seat. Her drink is over. She silences her buzzing phone and presses a few buttons on it. I take a moment to sip my drink and drink in our surroundings. The shop is busier and noisier than before as people of all age groups occupy every single chair. Really, I can't spot a single empty chair in my field of vision.

Neha starts again. "When do you plan to tell our parents?"

I shrug in response.

Wow. I have no plan of action in mind so far and thus, no answer to Neha's question; but her asking me this matter of fact signifies progress to me. As if we're in this together. As if she has understood and accepted the problem and is now strategising a way to go about it.

In my opinion, there are two types of people when it comes to dealing with problems. First, there are the people who take a lot of time and effort to acknowledge and accept a problem, then spend all their energies in fretting and fuming over the occurrence and misfortune of the situation, determining what caused it and whether there is a chance that it may not have actually happened. After all this, they finally get down to dealing with the difficulty. The second kind of people, who may also be as affected in the said situation as the first kind, act relatively less panicked and immediately shift focus to tackling the issue, keeping all their whining and worrying for later. More often than not, this also helps them cope better with the situation as the initial shock is absorbed and overshadowed by keeping the mind busy. Neha has proved more than once that she belongs to the second group of people and I'm really beginning to like her nature.

"You tell me," I throw the ball in her court, "When do you think we should tell everyone? I want to do this as soon as possible. It doesn't feel...."

"Whoa whoa whoa! Wait a minute," Neha cuts me short. "There's no **'we'** in this situation, Nikhil. If you're thinking of calling off this wedding then you're going to have to break the news to our parents on your own. This is not **my** decision, it's yours. I can't even afford to tell my parents that I know about it."

Oh. So we're not in this together. I realise that my surreptitious attempt to make this 'break-up affair' look mutual has not succeeded. The way Neha said what she said makes me wonder if at all she is also under any pressure to get married, but looking at her family I don't think so. My aim to make things look mutual was not only so that we could share the blame but also share the contempt. In fact, I had thought about this more for the benefit of Neha, thinking about her prospects in the future. A mutual break-up gives the benefit of the doubt to both parties. It's so much better than one person leaving the other, from the perspective of the one who gets left. But Neha's stern resolve has made it amply clear to me that she will not lend her name to this decision.

Fair enough.

"Ya ya, don't worry," I immediately quip despite being very worried myself. "I'm just asking for your suggestion. When do you think will be a good time to tell them?"

"I don't know. Is there ever a good time for bad news?"

Neha has a flourishing way with words. Media is her thing, no wonder!

"I suggest you don't waste any time. The final invitation sample will definitely come by tomorrow. You should tell them before it goes for printing."

I notice her voice fade; almost break with every word she utters, as if she's just actually realising the enormity of what's happening right now.

"Oh God, Nikhil, is this actually happening?" she says in a low-pitched, choked voice reaching out for my hand and lightly grasping it. Who would have thought that the same words a girl usually utters when she is getting married, can be uttered in the exactly opposite situation as well? I'm momentarily paralysed by the sudden change in Neha's emotion.

"You're **actually** breaking this engagement?" she says, more to convince herself than ask me. "Really, why are you doing this, Nikhil?" she squeezes my hand and utters. Her eyes fill with tears which threaten to fall but she blinks them away, trying her best to hold herself together.

Gone is the poised, all-in-control, undeterred and confident Neha. Here is a girl weakened by circumstance, exposing her fear and vulnerability in a situation which is out of her hands, to which she has made no contribution, but which she must bear the consequences of.

In the few seconds after she utters these words and before I start to uselessly apologise I feel a gut-wrenching pain, a sickening guilt in my conscience. Still stumped and paralysed I feel tremendously sorry for her and tremendous hatred for myself; actual hatred of a kind that would not be forgotten for a long time if it were for another human being. I feel so sorry and responsible that she has to go through this because of my selfish and visceral decision. My stomach churns and the little bit of drink I have consumed threatens to reroute itself upward as I lifelessly look into those sad, questioning, piercing eyes.

"I'm so sorry, Neha," I plead in a small and emasculated voice, my head drooping, my body leaning forward as I try to contain my own emotions. I wedge her proffered hand between both mine and implore her to forgive me giving her moist palm a reassuring squeeze, though I can guarantee she receives no reassurance. Can anybody blame her?

"You don't even want to **think** about it? Give it some time? How are you so sure?" she asks in incredulity, retracting her arm and flopping both her hands on her lap.

I look away towards the floor on my right wishing for the **first** time that I'd never met Aarti. I thought it would never come to this but seeing Neha here, like this, because of me, is making me realise that if I'd never come across Aarti we would not be here right now.

Why did I have to feel like this towards Aarti? Why did she have to come to the engagement? Why couldn't she have directly come to our wedding? Or would that have been worse? Would I have broken my marriage because of what I feel for her? Maybe not, but again how can I know until I'm in that situation? Although I do know that if I were already married to Neha and happened to feel something so strong towards another woman, I would not break my marriage before trying my best to save it. Then why am I not willing to do that now? Is it because it's not too late? Because engagement is not the finality that marriage is; because I still have this option, this one last chance. All along I looked at it as a blessing in disguise but right now as I sit here facing the victim of my circumstance I think it would have been better if I'd never met Aarti at all. And what am I even doing this for? It's not like Aarti is going to fall in love with me or marry me. Despite the small hope of possibility that I'm nursing, my rational self knows that

Aarti will most probably never love me back. Then why am I doing this at all?

Seeing Neha come undone like this on my account makes me think, for a nanosecond, if I shouldn't do this and should marry her as per promise. If I tried, really tried, I could forget all about Aarti and lead a normal, happy life with Neha. But the fact that Aarti is on my mind even in this heart-breaking situation is enough reason for me to dismiss the thought immediately.

"At least tell me **WHY?**" Neha's morose voice rightfully demands. I break my long, hypnotic 'eye-contact' with the floor and sheepishly look at Neha without an answer.

"I deserve to know, Nikhil," she asserts. "It's just sinking in, that you're breaking this relationship. In fact, it had just started to sink in that we're getting married and now…." she says and looks away with a jerk, as if looking at me is too painful, as if looking at me repulses her. I too want to tear my gaze away from her but she's commanding every fragment of my attention right now. I'm just so sorry about this situation.

"I… I.. I can't apologise enough. No amount of sorry will be enough for what I'm doing. I don't know what to say Neha."

"Just tell me why! I deserve to know," she reiterates the fact, leaning in and firmly grasping the table.

"I've already told you; you know why," I say vaguely as I feel the temperature of my neck, ears and cheeks rise again.

"No, I don't. I can't believe the rubbish reasons you're giving me. Even if there's any truth to them I can't believe that you would want to break our engagement because of that. Even when I felt all the things you said you felt about not having anything special I never thought of leaving you. It's so drastic, what you're doing. For God's sake Nikhil, we just got engaged two weeks ago! What the hell happened that you want to leave me suddenly?" she says, her voice rising a few octaves. The shrillness of her pitch makes me jumpy and alarmed, though no one around us seems to take notice. My conscience is now drowning in guilt as my mind races for words, and inside, I'm reeling from the whirlwind of emotions Neha is making me feel with herself.

"Have I been such a bad partner to you that I don't even deserve a reason; an answer? No closure?" she says moping.

"Stop it, please. Don't say it like that."

"Not saying it won't change it. What you've said to me… is it really just that? Or is something else bothering you? Or is it something you can't tell me? Something I've done?"

"No no no. It's nothing you've done, Neha. Please. I've told you this."

"Then?"

Silence ensues for a few seconds.

"Your silence is telling me a lot, Nikhil," she points out. "Please. Tell me. Stop me from thinking the worst. How am I supposed to deal with this without any justification? I'll go mad, Nikhil. Why are you doing this? At least just tell me **why?**" she pleads, and for the first time in our meeting so far I fear that she's really going to cry.

I'm at a complete loss. Resigned and helpless I stifle a sigh, place my elbows on the table and let my forehead slump on my fingers. I'm like that child who covers his face with the belief that it will make him and his surroundings disappear.

"**That** bad, huh?" Neha gathers. "Come on, Nikhil. I mean how bad could it be? You've already made your decision. The least you can do is tell me what happened."

She's absolutely right. It's the least and the worst I could do.

"Neha, please," I beseech her, letting my guard down. "I don't want to lie to you. Please don't make me do this right now. I'm begging you. Let it go."

"I'm begging you too. You've just confirmed my doubts. How can I let it go when I know you're hiding something from me? Put yourself in my place and see."

"I...it's complicated. I can't explain it in a way that you'll understand."

"You can at least try. Understanding it is my problem. Anyway you've already made your decision."

"Look, Neha. I'm sorry, but I really can't do this right now," I say firmly. How can I possibly tell her the whole truth?

"Wow! Thanks, Nikhil. After everything, you have the audacity to deny me the one thing I'm asking from you. For your sake I hope that you're ready to answer our families because, believe me, they **will** want a concrete reason," she says exasperatedly.

I'm ready to face any mockery, disdain and taunts that Neha wants to throw at me so long as she lets this subject go. She pointedly looks away from me again.

"I guess we're done here then. Let's leave. Thanks for coffee," she says gathering her belongings and making to leave.

"Neha, **wait**," I holler, reaching across and stopping her by the hand. She pauses and listens. "Don't leave like this. I know I can't expect you to be normal but please don't leave in anger. I may not want this wedding but I really care for you and I'll never forgive myself for hurting you."

"What is the point of saying all this, Nikhil? Does it really matter? Let's just leave…. And you're right; you can't expect me to be normal. At least allow me the right to be as I want. You can't have everything, you know. You deserve all the guilt you're feeling."

I ignore her acerbic remarks, grateful that she's still seated, and try a different approach.

"Yes. Yes, I do. Please just sit here with me till I finish my drink. Five minutes. We won't talk if you don't want to. I just can't let you leave like this. Please."

She lets out a loud breath, releases her bag from her grasp and places it down, then stares at me, her eyes boring into mine as if she's trying to search my brain and read my mind.

I'm a bundle of nerves as I take unwelcome swigs of my remaining drink. She involuntarily and gradually eases out of her bad temper and absentmindedly takes in our surroundings. I don't know what we're actually doing here right now; maybe just cooling off? Whatever it is, it's working. I'm not nearly as shaky as I was just moments ago and I allow myself to feel slightly relieved and triumphant.

I've sat through it after all. The major hurdle has been crossed.

I place my empty cup down on the table with a slightly louder thud in order to signify to her that I'm done. Our meeting has progressed to its end. I'm not sure if she's got her car to work today but I'm about to offer dropping her home anyway when she says, "Is there someone else?"

CHAPTER 28

Fuck. Weren't we done? What the hell prompted her to say this? I'm numb with shock at her question. What do I say to that? 'Yes, yes there is a girl I want to marry but she has not the slightest idea of my intentions, and here's an interesting fact – she's your best friend.' Should I say this? Or should I say 'no' knowing that it will make me a liar in my own eyes despite the fact that I'm not seeing anybody.

There are so many things I can say right now but my conscience doesn't allow me to utter a single word for fear of speaking lies or saying the truth, neither of which shall benefit me.

After the ten-twelve seconds that I've just stared at her, something strikes Neha and half-covering her mouth she gasps, **"Oh shit, Nikhil! You're seeing someone!"** Her face is marked by sheer horror. "Shit shit! How could I not have seen this? Of course!" she almost squeals.

"No, no no!" I blurt out reactively. "You're getting it all wrong Neha. I'm not seeing anybody." This much is true.

"Lies! All bloody bullshit. It all makes sense. God! I'm such an idiot. You probably never wanted to marry me! Shit.... **How could you do this to me**? My family? Why, Nikhil?" she says disbelievingly. **"Fuck,"** she swears as an afterthought.

"Neha, **listen** to me," I demand firmly. "Don't jump to wrong conclusions. Like you and your family already know, I **am** single. I've been single for the past two years. My last girlfriend was my neighbour in Manchester and things were not at all serious with her. Even my mother knows this. They would be okay if I wanted to marry anyone of my choice.... And trust me, even if I had a girlfriend and my parents didn't accept her, I would never purposely use your family like this. I am **not** seeing anybody," I conclude, frustrated and exasperated.

"Then why didn't you say anything when I asked you?"

I say nothing.

"*Haan?*" she prods.

Nothing again.

"You're just playing with words, Nikhil. Just stop it now. I'm not a fool. I think I sensed something yesterday only but it didn't strike me. Never in my life would I have guessed this until you told me!"

I just can't do this anymore.

"Tell me, Nikhil, without trying to change the subject. Am I wrong?"

I'm stupefied. Ideally, I should lie to her and get out of here. End this discussion for now. But something nagging won't let me. I don't know what comes over me to say what I say.

"No.... No, you're not wrong. I... I," words fail me as they often do these days. I resign myself to the situation, tired of planning my words and plotting my actions. I've always lived my life in 'reaction-mode', never having to weigh what I say or do. It's the best way to live when you have no secrets to protect, and liars will never know the bliss of such a carefree life.

I stop thinking and shut my overactive mind and the voice in my head that's constantly barking moves at me, giving me too many options at every point.

"I knew it!" she says and sits back almost victoriously.

"But I'm **not** having an affair," I point out one last time.

"What is it then? I know you're not gay," she says warily, cautiously eyeing me as if to confirm.

What is it with people thinking I'm gay? I want to laugh and scream at the same time.

"You're right. I'm not."

"Then what is it? What is your big secret? Spit it out already," she says frustrated and tired. Her anger has subsided again as curiosity takes over.

"Neha, let's leave *yaar*! Aren't you sick of all this? Let's just go."

"As soon as you tell me, we'll leave," she pesters.

"Fine! I think I'm in love with someone," I lash out and look away, exceptionally annoyed and agitated.

Take that and **bite me**! Kill me if you want to!

When I look back at her after a few seconds she's staring at me intently, her lips slightly parted, examining and scrutinising my face as if I'm a museum art piece; as if she cannot comprehend what I am.

"What? Say something, please."

She takes a deep breath. "I... I don't know what to say; how to feel. I'm just so confused right now."

I summon a waiter with my hand and with only gestures ask him to bring me a glass of water. My throat is dry like a desert.

"With who?" she urges. 'With whom' I want to correct her, but again it's hardly appropriate. I blink wordlessly.

"Since when? Since when is this going on?" she asks and before I can answer, continues, "Why aren't you marrying her then?.... I….. I just have so many questions."

"I can understand, Neha but…." I pause to form a complete sentence in my head before I speak it.

"Wait," she cuts me anyway, "You said your parents don't have any issues if you choose a girl to marry. Then? Then why all this? I'm not understanding anything. Will you please explain things to me once and for all, Nikhil?"

And in a jiffy it's clear to me that there's just no point in playing hide and seek anymore; just no point in prolonging my own agony, and that of Neha's. I should let things take their own course. So much has revealed itself already.

"It's only very recent, Neha. That I've realised this…felt this way. None of this was a plan. Trust me on this."

"So you're saying you realised you love her after meeting me?"

"Yes."

"Wow! And what about her? She didn't stop you from marrying me? Or she doesn't feel the same way about you?"

I feel my pulse quicken, my body perspire, my breath rise. With immense courage I continue to be honest.

"Neha, I've just met her. This is not one of my exes. I met her much after our families met for our marriage talks."

She's too startled as she wraps her head around this piece of information and I feel like I've stopped breathing, totally aware that any minute now my deepest, darkest secret shall be exposed.

"**Who** is this girl?" she utters just like I had anticipated, but in spite of expecting the question, hearing her say it in reality is like having my worst fears come alive.

As I told you earlier, the one and only time I'd failed a subject in school I was frightened to death about my parents' reactions. I had spent hours reciting perfectly thought-out lines, which my naïve mind conjured up to tell my parents when I would have to explain myself. But when the time came and when I was confronted, nothing even remotely close to what I had prepared came out of my mouth. This is just like that, except that it's worse.

"**Damn it**, Nikhil! Tell me."

"I can't," I say simply.

"What do you mean you **can't**? You **have** to tell me….. And how does it even matter now? And I don't even know half your people."

It's not any of my people; it's yours. If only I was courageous enough to directly tell her...

"You're making me very nervous. Just say it. Have I met her?"

I nod reluctantly, my gaze fixed on the ground, my mind and heart exploding.

"**When?**" she exclaims. "Was she at our engagement Nikhil?"

I nod again, wiping a bead of sweat above my brows. I can almost taste the tension radiating between us.

"But.... One second; none of your girl friends were at the engagement," she recalls with a little difficulty. "Except that one family friend of yours. Obviously not **her** right?"

Obviously! The girl is what, **17?**

"There was that other girl also, in the blue outfit, but she's related to you in some way right?" Neha keeps up her guessing. Trust girls to remember the colour of another girl's outfit even on their deathbed!

"It's none of my friends, Neha," I clarify, almost willing her to figure it out.

"Huh?" she expresses her confusion.

Then, her eyebrows shoot up in extreme alarm and her eyes protrude noticeably as she stiffens.

"**What are you saying?**" she says giving each word equal emphasis. "Are you saying you're in love with one of **my** friends?"

I look away, too embarrassed to face her, allowing her to continue her calculations. She rightly takes my silence as agreement.

After about six excruciating seconds, she says, "Shreya?" in a confused, disbelieving and doubtful way as if to say, 'How's that possible?'

It's no surprise that Shreya is her first guess considering she is the epitome of good looks, but surely Neha knows that Sid and Shreya are having a scene.

And then…. She clutches the table almost as if for support and reaching for her mouth with one hand, in slow motion, full Hindi-film style if I may add, she guesses, "**Aarti**!"

If I didn't know better, I would've thought my heart had stopped at this moment. Shock, utter shock is scraped on Neha's whole face, her whole body actually. She knows. She now knows it's Aarti that I'm in love with.

It's all happened under a minute from when she started her calculation. Her guessing quickly escalated into judgment even as I neither denied nor accepted anything; just implored her to reach here on her own. When I dare to look at her face she's squinting into my eyes.

"**Aarti?**" she says this time with intonation, pure bewilderment and victimisation etched on her face.

My stomach roils.

"**Say it, damn it**," she hollers, even though she knows it's true.

I lower my eyes from hers at first, then with a faint nod, I look upward again, scared for dear life. I'm sure I look like I'm about to cry or shit my pants but I won't do either.

Suddenly, in a move that I did not see coming, Neha springs up from her seat, unintentionally or not, jolting the table slightly towards me. With seething agony she flings her right arm in the air then clutches her forehead with it and yells, **"What the fuck?"**

A few moments ago, I may have subconsciously noticed that the one man sitting on the only table close to ours had abandoned his headphones in favour of our conversation. It hadn't bothered me that he was overhearing us but right now, as Neha towers above me lashing out at my unpleasant disclosure, I can spot at least three successive tables' worth of people gaping at us, all highly entertained. Apart from them there's a waiter and a cleaner, both diligently engrossed and amused. Despite this, I'm thankful to myself for not having taken a more centralised table.

I have nothing to say to Neha as she lurches accusations at me, one after another in full public view. My mental machinery has tentatively put her out of focus, totally zoomed her out as I look at our audience, some of which pretends not to eavesdrop when I look at them.

"Hello!" she shakes the table slightly, leaning in, to get my attention. "Since when is this going on? **This is just so wrong, Nikhil,**" she pounds her fist on the table, almost in sobs but somehow still holding herself together. I hope more than anything right now that she doesn't cry. I won't know what to do with her if she does. Crying women make me very nervous and uncomfortable.

"Nothing is going on, Neha; **for God's sake**, how many times do I have to say that?"

"Oh please! **Enough** with your bullshit," she exclaims, using her hands for added-effect as she straightens herself.

After a few seconds of chewing on the astonishing fact that I'm in love with Aarti, Neha starts nodding vigorously, swinging her head from side to side as if she's feeling enormous pity for herself. Her face is contorted with despair and misery.

"**That bitch**," she says with malice.

What? Who? What?

My eyes shoot up to her demonstrating how startled I am by her words. Sure, I'm a bitch, but I think she's referring to Aarti. Why? What has Aarti done in this whole situation? I think Neha is convinced that Aarti and I are involved in some sort of clandestine relationship, in spite of my efforts to convince her otherwise. Surprisingly she has no faith in her own best friend. Not having faith in me is understandable; I've proved it with my own admission that I don't deserve it. But to doubt **Aarti** like this?

"I **knew** it! I knew she was not worthy of my friendship. I should have **never** trusted her," Neha asserts to nobody in particular. At this point she's just having a monologue of sorts.

I just don't understand this reaction of hers. Her vehemence towards me I can understand and tolerate but the intensity with which she is reprimanding Aarti has me surprised. There's probably more to their friendship than meets the eye, which I've definitely worsened. I think of Neha's relationship with her friends, as she rambles on in front of me, but no obvious signs of a problem come to mind immediately; until now of course. But then again how long have I known Neha to know about her relationships with her friends? One thing has always been clear though; that Neha is more affectionate towards Shreya than Aarti, but that's hardly a problem. And I'm obviously wrong. Something is amiss.

I involuntarily feel defensive towards Aarti, not only because I love her but more importantly because she has nothing to do with this; nothing and yet everything, but nothing of her own accord. The poor girl has no idea of the bills I'm encashing on her account. She's going to hate me. The thought is repulsive.

"Neha, she has nothing to do with this," I somehow muster the courage to say on Aarti's behalf.

"Oh ya? I'm sure you would know..... Shit man.... How, Nikhil? How **could** you do this? How could you both do this? You know nothing about her. She ... I feel so cheated and disgusted." With just her expression, Neha exudes such abhorrence that my mind is plagued with guilt and aversion for myself even more than it already is.

After a few seconds of no words, she rapidly assembles her things with more vigour than is needed for such a negligible task, then turns on her foot and makes her way towards the exit of the coffee shop, unbothered by our viewers.

As soon as it dawns on me that Neha is walking out, I bolt upright and call after her, ready for a chase. Stopping a few steps ahead she sharply turns in my direction and raising her palm towards me warns, "**Don't,**" with such extreme wrath that it's enough to freeze me to my spot and let her go.

With a flourish she exits the place, making me the sole subject of public scrutiny now. How short-sighted I was to think that we were going to do this in a dignified and mature manner! But fair enough. Certain deeds and situations deserve no dignity.

I contemplate following her, despite her explicit instruction not to, then decide against it, for I have nothing more to say to her; no way to offer her any comfort. She has to come to terms with this on her own and nagging her will not help. And besides, we've put up enough of a show already. I could do without another public spat for a few years.

I'm sceptical about my conduct now in front of my keen observers as I step back to my table.

Be cool. I'm sure this happens all the time. Just be cool, I tell myself. Should I just leave too? I never have to look at these people again in my life, so why do I feel the need to explain myself to them? I'm a good guy, I promise, I want to tell all of them but obviously I don't.

Temporarily, I take my seat at the table that Neha has just abandoned. My untouched glass of water rests on it and for lack of any activity I decide to down it, though I'm not sure if my body will accept any intake at the moment. The water is a surprising relief and a sympathetic waiter even offers me another glass, which I decline. I'm fine. Move on, you guys! This is not a big deal, really! Except, that it is.

Since ordering another item will be pushing it too far I decide to make a quick, hasty exit with as little attention on me as possible. Most people have now turned away from my direction and are doing their own thing. I stand up from my chair, and pretending to call someone on my phone, nonchalantly exit the coffee shop, genuinely hoping that for the rest of my life I don't come across anybody who witnessed my emasculation today

CHAPTER 29

As I step out of the coffee house I'm momentarily dazed and disoriented. I stroll towards my car which is parked close by, with no clue what to do now, or where to go. I'm utterly confused what my successive actions should be after my awful encounter with Neha.

Should I wait for her to report our altercation to her parents? No.

Should I own up to her parents myself? No, for I can't possibly flout the decision to marry their daughter in front of them, and that too without the awareness and approval of my own parents.

Then should I own up to my parents first? Maybe. This seems like the only executable option at this point, though I'm sure that no matter how well I execute it, my parents will not accept my decision.

Maybe it's time I tell them the real reason I want to do this. Maybe it's time I tell them about Aarti before Neha does. I fear this the most, just like I feared my class teacher telling my parents that I'd failed before I could.

Out of frustration I bang my fist on the steering wheel. It stings! The parking conductor hovers around me waiting for me to pay his due parking charges. Without bothering to ask how much I owe him I shove a fifty in his hand and take whatever denomination he returns along with a slip. I add it all to the petty cash collection at the console of my car, which my dad mainly maintains for quick change, and occasionally for paupers.

I then take a rather long and senseless route back home, sweating profusely throughout the way despite using the AC. For some unknown reason I'm in a hurry and yet reluctant to reach home. The minute I enter my building I abandon my imperfectly parked car and take the stairs, two at a time, to my house. On ringing the bell Kunta lets me in with her usual disinterest in life.

When I walk into the living area the sight of my parents casually chatting away over cups of tea and their favorite *bhel* both relieves my nerves and warms my heart at the same time. Their pleasant demeanour tells me that they know nothing yet. This is probably why I wanted to rush home; to see this normalcy, to see that everything is okay. Soon, this ease and relaxation on their face shall be wiped out and I will be solely responsible for it.

I plan to greet them briefly and dash into my room; take a bath maybe. The comfort of a long, soothing bath shall do me good.

"*Aa gaya* Nikhil?" my father says. I've always found this amusing of my parents; to sort of ask if someone has arrived upon their actual arrival. Obviously, if I'm in front of you I have arrived. But I don't think they mean to ask literally. It's mostly just a way of acknowledging.

"*Aaja, bhel khayega*?" my mother offers, pushing the plate of snacks towards me. Then she frowns and asks why I didn't eat my lunch at home. "*Nikhil dupahar main khaana kyun nahi khaaya? Waise ke waise hi pada tha.*"

"Sorry mom, wasn't hungry," I say and walk towards my room. Mom calls after me.

"*Aloo gobi banayi thi.* Will you eat that for dinner? Otherwise, say what you want."

"I'll eat that only."

"You went out to eat?"

I nod.

"With Neha?"

I nod again, despite knowing that this will mislead them to imagine that Neha and I were on an actual 'date.'

"*Arre waah!*" My mother is all smiles. "You should have told me *na*. I would not have made lunch. Next time inform me or Kunta."

"Last minute plan *tha,*" I say and without giving them the chance to talk again I disappear into my room.

Within minutes I'm in my bathroom, staring at my face in the mirror. I have no idea how many minutes pass as I stand deliberating, just as I have no idea what time it is right now. The more I stare at myself the more I realise that this exercise is debilitating my spirits rather than lifting them. Sloshing my face with water I tell myself that there is no point in dwelling on things now. What's done is done.

I start stripping for a bath and when I'm not even halfway done my mother knocks on the door.

"Nikhil," she calls out startling me. When you've done something you're not proud of even the slightest thing is enough to make you jump out of your skin.

"Nikhil," she calls again. It's not like her to call after someone who is in the washroom unless it's urgent, so she has me worried.

"Ya mom. I'm having a bath."

"Oh. *Beta*, your phone is ringing nonstop. Should I pick it up?"

Fuck. Mindlessly I reverse my undressing process at the speed of light. Who would be calling me? In some part of my mind I get the horrible feeling that it's Neha. Actually, I know it's her. Shit, this can't be good.

What will I say to her? What if mom picks up and Neha tells her everything?

"Why are you having a bath at this time?" she asks across the door. I can faintly hear my ringtone now.

"I'm coming out. Don't answer the call," I tell her nervously. In haste I button down my shirt asymmetrically and spring out of the bathroom.

When I enter my room it's abuzz with the sound of my phone and my mother is picking it up. Without any thought, and almost reactively I scuttle across to her and wrest my phone out of her grasp. My ninja-like move prevents her from seeing the identity of my caller, which I don't see either. I loll my phone-held hand beside me effectively concealing the screen and click on the side to silence the incessant ringing. Anxious and agog, I feel like an adolescent boy who's been caught by his mother indulging in some impermissible activity like smoking or watching porn.

My mother looks at me, offended and quizzical at once. I know I'll have to explain myself for my petulant action so before she says anything I mutter, "Sorry mom, I'm expecting some urgent call from office."

"Really? Are you sure, *beta*?" she feigns suspicion.

"Ya. Obviously," I tell her unconvincingly.

"It looks like you're hiding something, Nikhil. You're scaring me too much nowadays."

"Relax, mom. I've got to take this call okay?" I say hoping she'll leave the room now.

"You didn't even see who's calling." She's ready to get to the bottom of this.

"Shalini," my father summons her. Thank you papa! At this point he's a godsend.

My mother narrows her eyes at me and pouts knowing that this is perhaps the end of my interrogation.

My phone starts to ring audibly again and it takes a monumental effort on my part not to instantly check who is calling me. Giving me the looks, mom walks across me and going out of the room says, "*Utha le. Maine waise bhi tere chakkarro mein nahi padna.*"

She exits the room and my world collapses when I see the name of my caller. You can take a guess at who it is, but not even for a ridiculous moment did I have the foresight to know that this would be happening. I'm hit by a wave of nausea as a blizzard of thoughts and questions cross my mind. **Why would Aarti be calling me right now?**

CHAPTER 30

I'm at the threshold of my house when Aarti's call stops ringing again. The unpredictability of this conversation is not suitable for the confines of my house. In a state of panic and fear I run down to the no-man's land between the fifth and fourth floor staircase of my building. The space offers me the silence, secrecy and anonymity I need right now.

In the past I've conducted all sorts of impermissible activities like the ones I spoke of earlier on the landing between the eight floor and the terrace of my building. Our terrace was a locked-down, seldom-used space throughout my school years and has remained so to date. That space has housed several memorable experiences for me including my first kiss, followed by many others.

Presently, when I check my phone it tells me that I have missed three calls from Aarti. Really, why would she be calling me?

There could be numerous reasons for her to contact me but the astonishing probability of the one reason I fear the most is bone-chilling. I'm torn between the idea of calling her back or not, or calling Neha, or heading straight to the airport. I think that would be best.

Confirming to myself the possibility that Aarti now knows everything, I inwardly curse myself for not expecting this and not having taken any pre-emptive measures to brace myself for it. This is the worst way for Aarti to find out that I love her. In hindsight, telling Neha everything does seem like a hare-brained decision, but even in retrospection I can't think of any other way in which I could have dealt with the situation. It was inevitable.

I check my phone again. It's 4:56pm and a good three minutes since Aarti's last call. After some fruitless pacing, with a racing heartbeat, damp shirt and dampened spirit I click on her number. It's best to face this once and for all. I have no idea what to expect or how to go about this but I'm determined to call Aarti back. With sheer bravery I press the 'call' button.

I involuntarily pay particular attention to the noise of the frequency wave after dialling. My breath picks up speed when the phone starts ringing. Aarti answers on the third ring.

"**Nikhil**?" she says in a way that crushes the tiny hope that I nursed that maybe, just maybe this was about something else.

Believe it or not, I note that this is the first time I've heard Aarti say my name. How odd, both the fact that she hadn't uttered it on any occasion before and the fact that I should have this realisation now, in **this** situation.

"Hi, Aarti," I say cautiously, nervously.

"Nikhil, what the hell man? What did you tell Neha? She... she just called me and said such unbelievably disgusting things to me. 'I' tried to 'seduce' you? **Really**? **When**?" she bombards me.

Seduce? What the hell?

"What?"

"Yes! And she said that you yourself have admitted this. I... Yuck! This is so ridiculous and embarrassing...... I thought it was a joke first but she was crying and yelling on the phone."

"Shit. Look..."

"She said I'm **jealous** of her; of you both and I'm trying to come in the middle and take revenge on her because of our fallout in the past. Really, is she crazy? And you're crazy too if you've ever felt that I've tried to **flirt** with you. Crazy and delusional. What is going on?" she asks sternly. She sounds mighty angry and offended and possibly hurt; naturally.

I feel an irrational surge of anger towards Neha. Yes, I wronged her, but she has overstepped the mark by telling Aarti what I'm hearing; painting a completely false picture. This is all preposterous. How can Neha accuse Aarti of **seducing** me? She doesn't know squat about the situation. How can she be so impulsive? Like I'm one to talk!

"Hello? Nikhil?"

"Aarti, I'm so sorry. I can explain," I offer in a small voice. I'm shamefaced at this exposé and sure that my face has turned red. My insides are on fire and not in a good way. The one person I think I may truly be in love with is on the verge of hating me right now. I have not felt a greater sadness in my life than this.

"**What**?" she snaps. "You mean all this **actually** happened? I... I was still thinking it's possibly a joke. **What the hell**?"

"This is a misunderstanding. Let me explain."

"Okay. I'm listening," she challenges angrily.

I go mute. I have so much to say and yet nothing to speak.

"Tell me Nikhil. What has happened that your fiancé, who happens to be my **closest** friend, has called me up blaming me for breaking her engagement, which by the way I was not even aware of? I'd **really** like to know how **I** did this."

"Aarti I'm **really** sorry you had to hear all this. I know you haven't done anything. Can we... can we please meet somewhere?" I'm uttering words spontaneously as they come unbidden to my mind.

"And how would that help?"

"Please. I need to explain myself to you. Please Aarti, give me **one chance** to tell you everything. I **have** to meet you," I plead.

"So that tomorrow Neha can accuse me of meeting you behind her back, having an affair with you? No, thank you. Whatever you have to say, say it now."

"Just five minutes, Aarti. I'll never be able to live with myself."The need in my voice is betraying my hold. I cannot believe what I'm feeling right now.

"No, Nikhil. Just **tell me** what's going on man.... I'm really sorry you guys are having problems but why am I being dragged into it? I have never ever looked at you in any way apart from my friend's husband. I'm disgusted by what I've heard."

My heart metaphorically cracks into a million shards at her words. I'm sure this is the worst day I'll ever live.

There are pools of water in my eyes and even Aarti sounds emotional right now but not as angry as she was earlier.

"I **never** told Neha that you seduced me, or that you tried to break our engagement. Believe me," I say, effectively masking the whole truth, but honestly nevertheless.

"So she just made it up? **For fun**? Why would she randomly lie like that? This is a pretty serious accusation..... You know what, Nikhil, you seemed like a really nice guy when I first met you. If you and Neha were having problems and you didn't have a way out you didn't have to use my name... You know, she felt that I was one of the reasons for her break up with Gaurav... when I had no bloody hand in it and now she's blaming me for this as well. At least with Gaurav there was some history! I could understand her anger... But you? I don't even know you! How can she possibly think this? I can't believe I have to prove myself all over again. After ages I felt that our friendship was finally stable. And now..." she sniffs.

Gaurav! The same fellow Neha was talking about. All this sudden information is just too much to process. I'm shocked. I think of Neha's anger in the coffee shop and now I get where it was coming from. I wish I had known about all this but I assume it's irrelevant at this point. I've made Aarti seem like a culprit in Neha's eyes. A tear falls astray from my right eye when I realise that she's crying. She continues.

"I've heard enough. Maybe Neha and my friendship is just jinxed. After everything, all these years, this is what I get? A bunch of **crappy** accusations that have no truth to them? I don't even know where this is coming from. And suppose it's true; even if you said those things and I did do that, she didn't even bother to clarify with me, check with me, and let me explain.... I'm just done trying. To hell with you guys," she hangs up.

So **that's** how I shall have to remember my first ever phone conversation with Aarti.

I stand hypnotised, paralysed and motionless for a few moments after Aarti hangs up on me, trying hard to adjust to the magnificence of what just happened. And then a natural instinct we all know too well makes me run like a mad man. I leap up to my door, ring the bell vociferously and an unnecessary number of times. Kunta is confused and annoyed at letting me in for a second time in a matter of minutes. I rush past her, straight to the guest bathroom, which is the closest bathroom to the main door and upon reaching I spew out a great deal of my intake in the last twenty hours or so. It's not a very beautiful sight so I shan't elaborate on it further.

After fifteen uncomfortable minutes I exit the bathroom feeling too empty, too weak and dog-tired. It's like I've been physically labouring and toiling, lifting ridiculously heavy weight. I think we underestimate the weight of the mind. My focus is just on my immediate feelings and surroundings right now. I contemplate sprawling on the ugly bed in the guest bedroom that has never seemed this inviting to me. But knowing Kunta, she would definitely have informed my mother that I've come home again who will wonder when I left in the first place. I figure that I have some more explaining to do.

Craftily, and with the least effort possible I open the guest bedroom door to check if the coast is clear. I'm acting like a thief in my own house. My plan is to quietly abscond the house for a little while; get some fresh air and a fresh perspective on things. I don't have long before I'll have to tell my parents about breaking the engagement with Neha and so I need to plan that as well. The revelation shall be a post-dinner affair tonight.

There's no one outside the room as I start to tip-toe my way to the main door. I've almost made it scot-free when Kunta confronts me about my absurd behaviour.

"*Bhaiya*," she calls out. Damn. So close man; so close.

The main door is ajar and I hold on to it. "*Haan?*"

"*Madamji bulla rahi hai. Aap woh room mein kya dhoond rahe the?*" she asks, wondering what I was doing in a room that I seldom enter.

Her pronunciation of 'madamji' is not what it should be, just like the word itself. Its sounds like may-dum-jee.

"*Kuch nahi. Mummy ko bolo thodi der mein aa raha hoon. Sid ko milne jaa raha hoon,*" I lie. Just like in college, using Sid as an excuse to get out of the house always comes handy.

Kunta has been with us since Before Christ so she knows almost all the people associated with us on first and pet name basis.

I scurry out of the house before she can say anything else. I'll explain things to mom later. I should note down the number of things I'm going to have to explain to her tonight.

As if it's a natural process I head straight to the corner of my lane which houses a small *paan-bidee* shop. Without any exchange of words, Milind, the shop owner hands me a Marlboro Gold and takes the change I offer.

Milind has been my go-to guy ever since my secret smoking days in childhood. I know it was not a very clever and secretive idea to buy cigarettes in my very own lane for fear of being caught but because I was almost always aware of my parents' whereabouts I used to do it anyway. After buying the cigarettes every one or two days I would go to the next lane or to the top of my building and smoke. The first few times I bought a cigarette were very scary. I would constantly be scanning the surroundings for the few seconds that the transaction would last. Milind's shop is adjoining a number of other household shops, like the dairy my mom patronises, the grocery store she can't do without, the chemist that has relieved us at odd hours of the day. The shops are so crammed next to each other that to a passer-by it could look like I'm buying a packet of milk or a medicine whilst I was actually buying a smoke. After the first few attempts I had mastered the art of purchasing these little fellows. It took a few years to figure out my brand as I tried and tested the hard ones and the light ones, the fake ones and the original ones, Milind's recommendations every once in a while and my own findings of exotic foreign brands.

Over the years, our frequent association whenever I'm here has turned our relationship into a wordless exchange of acknowledgement and business.

After buying a few more cigarettes from him I smoke one right then and there; something I would not have done on a normal day, but right now I can't be bothered to think of consequences. At 29 I should be able to enjoy a vice without the fear of being scolded.

When I'm done I feel light-headed and slightly better. Smoking is my favourite way of de-stressing in distress. I have a ghost of an idea of what I want to do next, and an urgent need to do it. I get hold of my phone and dial a number.

CHAPTER 31

Sid picks up on the fifth ring. It's amazing how anxiety will make you notice things that you usually, subconsciously ignore.

"Bro, what's up?"

"Sid *sun*. I need a favour."

"*Haan, bol na. Abbe pehle bata* you met Neha? How did it go?"

"Not good man. It's messed up."

"Shit. What happened?"

"Fuck it *na*. I'll tell you all that later."

"Okay listen, I'll get done in fifteen twenty minutes. Let's meet for a beer?"

"No, not now. I have some work. Bro, I need a huge favour from you."

"*Arre haan,* tell me."

"*Nai pehle tu bol ke kaam karke dega.* I need your word on this."

"*Abbe* why you saying it like that?"

"Just say *na*."

"You know you're a chick sometimes. *Haan* I'll do it. *Ab bol*."

"Listen to me calmly. I **need you** to get me Aarti's exact address. **Somehow.** Don't ask me questions and all. Just please get it for me."

"**Are you crazy, Nikhil**? Why the hell do you want **Aarti's address?** What happened with Neha?"

"Sid man, chill. *Baat ko samajh.* Trust me it's urgent right now. Please bro, find out her address and give me *na*."

"No dude, I can sense that you're making a mistake. Nikhil don't do anything stupid in a hurry. First tell me what happened with Neha."

"I told her it's over. She went crazy. Figured it out about Aarti. I'm officially doomed. Now are you getting me the address or no?"

"How did she figure it out? You told her? Dude…"

"Not exactly. It's a long story."

"Uncle, Aunty know?"

"No, not yet."

"Shit man. This is serious shit."

"Fuck it now. I can't help it. Sid, bro I really need that address."

"*Nikhil, tu kya karne ki soch raha hai? Aarti ka address kyun chahiye? Bro iss waqt usse thoda door reh.* Don't do anything stupid."

I make an exasperated sound. Really, I am not a child.

"Siddharth trust me I know what I'm doing. Just fucking help me with the address man!"

It's funny how circumstances change people's position in your lives. When I first saw Aarti at my engagement I would never have thought that two weeks later I would be begging **Sid** of all people for **her** address. But right now he's the only one who can help me.

"*Yaar* how can I get her address anyway?"

"Ask Shreya."

"No dude; no way. I can't."

"Why not? See I already know she lives in Andheri. *Uss din yaad hai apni colony ke baare mein bol rahi thi?*"

"*Nahi, kab?*"

"*Accha woh sab chhod. Tu bas exact address find out kar.*"

"Bro," Sid sighs. "*Accha ruk main tujhe dus minute mein waapas call karta hoon. Boss bulla raha hai.*" Why the hell does this boss need him right this moment only?

"Okay, bye." We hang up.

Sid may not be able to fish out this questionable piece of information for me. This was a crucial part of my plan without which the rest of it is improbable. I quickly start on a 'Plan B.'

So I know the area that Aarti lives in since it had come up in conversation between her and Shreya on the way back from Pune, and even though I wanted to go all the way to drop her home that day she had alighted near the highway saying she's going somewhere else. Because I was overhearing the two girls talk I also know that Aarti has recently moved into a rented flat in a new society whose name I faintly recall.

Google tells me that there are at least six buildings in Andheri with the same name which is no surprise considering that Andheri is big enough to be a city by itself.

I may have to do the painful task of checking out each of these buildings if Sid can't get me the address but it's my best bet right now and one that I'm willing to take. But the problem I realise now is that even if I land up in the correct society there will be no way to know which building or flat is hers considering that she's a tenant.

Should I just call Shreya myself? It'll be painstakingly awkward for me to ask her for Aarti's address but actually she's the only one whom I can think of asking, because if I ask Neha or Aarti I might as well commit suicide.

On second thoughts, even if I do gather the courage to ask Shreya what reason will I give her for wanting Aarti's address? There's a chance she may immediately tell Neha or Aarti or both, and there's a chance that she may still not give me the address.

As I walk in slow motion towards my building from the curb I get that sinking feeling that totally deflates one's spirits when one realises that something exceptionally important in their life is falling apart and all they can do is haplessly watch.

My phone buzzes and I allow a tiny ray of hope to fill my mind.

"*Bol.*"

"*Haan,* sorry. *Dekh bhai maine Shreya ko call kiya, but bro bahut odd tha yaar.* I couldn't ask her man. **How to** ask her for Aarti's address? It looks so odd man. What will I say if she asks me why I want to know? Sorry bro, difficult *lag raha hai.*"

"*Yaar Sid, kuch bhi karke pooch na.* Take my name and ask; I don't care. I'm *toh* anyway screwed. Say, say Nikhil is asking."

"*Chal* suppose I say that also and she gives it to me. What if she immediately calls Neha, man? I'm sure you don't want that."

"Ya I know. So do something *na*. Make her swear that she won't tell anybody anything." Come on, it's high time we started using this favourite tactic of theirs on them. "Come on Sid, you should be able to make your girlfriend keep your secrets," I pump him.

"She's **not** my girlfriend," Sid protests. I want to challenge him on this but that's a conversation for another time, perhaps. There are only so many women-related issues a man can handle at a time!

"Okay, still. Can't you think of some way to get it out of her? Use my name and say you don't know why. **Please Sid.**"

"I don't know, man. I doubt it."

When I'm almost outside my building's gate I catch a glimpse of my father walking out of the lobby, and automatically retrace my steps. I can't deal with so many people right now. I dash into the neighbouring building and decide to stop pestering Sid.

"*Chal theek hai*. I'll manage. *Call karta hu tujhe baad mein,*" I say and hang up.

I see my father making his way out of my building for his evening walk and breathe a sigh of relief when he's out of sight.

Reluctantly, I admit to myself that realistically speaking, it would not have been so easy for Sid to get Aarti's address so I can't hold it against him. Ten minutes later he messages me the exact address.

I'm having another cigarette at Milind's when this happens. I think I might have physically jumped after at least two decades when I got Sid's message. It's not a full-fledged 'jumping jack' jump but let's just say it's not something you usually do at almost 30. I go through an instant reversal of the sinking feeling because of this little, tiny, impossible-to-get piece of information. Although I'm still in a major soup here, I allow myself to feel the optimism that a thin ray of sunshine can bring on a dark, gloomy, depressing day. It's my very own silver lining.

Before I get ahead of myself with all the philosophy and optimism, I remind myself that confronting Aarti and coming clean with her is not going to be a joyride or a memorable experience. Most people claim their love for someone with at least some assurance that their feelings will be reciprocated. I go into this fight knowing very well that it's a losing battle for me. And yet, doing this will rid me of the entire burden that secrecy has given me, all the load of lies and guilt. Even if Aarti hates me after this, I can't live another day without confessing my feelings for her, especially after our disastrous conversation.

I make a cursory call to Sid to thank him for his timely help. I now owe him big time he informs me. Then I leave Milind's spot.

I shift my mental and physical gear and within seconds I'm on my way to Aarti's place after purchasing a deodorant, some mint and a bottle of water. When I stop at the first red light after leaving my building it starts to drizzle. I take this as a good sign, even though I've never been superstitious in my life. I've come to realise that circumstance can play a huge role in shaping our beliefs. Sometimes circumstance can overpower plain simple logic as well. People become the way they are because of what they endure and experience.

I don't reactively roll up the window and allow the faint harmless drops of water into the car. An agitated commuter in the auto rickshaw next to me is not at all pleased by the mild shower. Both she and the rickshaw driver unanimously crib about the major increase in traffic that the rains cause in our city. He says 'traffic' in a very peculiar and interesting way, making it amply clear that he's a migrant. It sounds like the 'trophic' in 'catastrophic.'

By the time I'm at the next signal, the short-lived drizzle has faded away leaving behind a damp and cool but grey ambience.

It doesn't take too long or much of an effort to locate the society in which Aarti resides but convincing the suspicious gatekeeper to let me park my vehicle inside the premises is a trying conversation. I have to resort to bribery. On entering, when I see the vast expanse of the compound with more than necessary space for parking I have half a mind to go back and squabble with the fellow but I don't. "*Bahar ki gaadi allowed hi nahi hai*," he had said making it sound like a criminal offence.

There are five buildings lined equidistantly in the large compound and Sid's message tells me that Aarti resides in 'Block C' which is the middle one. After parking in a spot in front of her particular building I tidy myself and make my way to the lobby. The nameplate of flat no. 701 reads Mr. Bhambri. A slim and underfed, young-looking watchman rises from his table and gives me dubious looks when I'm scanning the name plates.

"*Kidhar jaana hai?*" he enquires, accosting me when I walk towards the lift. I want to tell him to mind his own business but then I also know that he's doing just that.

"*Saat mala; 701.*" I say confidently as if I come here every day.

"*Entry kariye book mein,*" he instructs me firmly gesturing towards an obviously placed log book that I hadn't noticed.

Obediently I fill out all the required basic information wondering if these details actually help in curbing crimes and nabbing criminals. I replace a few digits of my actual phone number in the last section of the page. He scrupulously reads the details and then nods approvingly. When I start to move again he says, "*Rukiye, intercom karna padega.*" My building has none of the latest security procedures in place so I'm not used to seeing this type of interrogation.

I feel irritated at the lengthy scrutiny but then mentally acknowledge that it's a good thing that Aarti is residing in such a responsible society, especially considering that she lives alone. As the watchman clings to the intercom receiver I examine him in detail. 'Nitin' his badge reads. His frail body and overtly hairy existence are enough for me to remember his palindromic name for the rest of my life. Suddenly I'm glad about his suspicion and extensive inspection and I want to thank him for being so protective of Aarti though I'm sure he does this for everybody in the building. I feel juvenile for my silly and irrelevant thoughts.

He puts the receiver down after a few seconds. "*Didi shayad abhi ghar pe nahi hai. Aap baad mein aaiye,*" he says and seats himself again, pointedly dismissing me.

Oh. Now what?

I can't do anything but wait till Aarti arrives from wherever she is because leaving this place without talking to her is not an option; that's if she's coming back at all. She could be in Kolkata with her parents for all I know.

I resort to playing Candy Crush on my phone for lack of anything better to do while I await my own doom.

Now that soon all of this commotion will come to an end, no matter what the outcome is, I'll be back to living my normal carefree life. There will be no need to run and hide; no need to plot and plan. Soon the burden of my impending wedding will officially be lifted from my shoulders and though I'm worried about my parents' reception of this news, I decide not to let it bog me down since it's not in my hands anymore. Whatever will be, will be.

In spite of preparing myself for the worst I'm kind of fascinated by the idea of finally telling Aarti that I love her.

Blocking all these worrisome thoughts from my mind I devote my complete attention to the game. Thirty-three long minutes are made bearable only because of this ridiculously enticing pastime. Then I have to stop because I've run out of virtual lives. A few messages await my attention but I know they can wait so I let them.

I decide I should probably call Aarti, just to gauge where she is without letting her know about my surprise visit, but I don't have the nerve to actually do it. My eyes have constantly been guarding the main gate of her society every few minutes since I've been waiting for her, noticing every single person walking in or out the premises. Apart from a few tall girls coming and going there hasn't been much activity. And then at precisely 7:04 pm an auto rickshaw parks outside the main entrance and a girl alights from it; a girl who I know is Aarti.

CHAPTER 32

I quickly down the remainder of my water while Aarti pays the rickshaw fare. I thought I'd reached the peak of my nervousness before meeting Neha today but that feeling doesn't come nearly as close to how nervous I am right now. All the confidence I managed to harbour with great difficulty so far has suddenly left my body and mind. She won't slap me, will she?

Although I could confine him to the floor with just one move, I comically picture an irate Nitin violently dragging me out of the building in full public view.

No, that won't happen; but I wonder what will.

Aarti reties her hair, then picks up two grocery bags from the rickshaw and enters the complex. My pulse involuntarily quickens. I wonder if I should meet her downstairs or let her go to her house and then follow. The latter will look too suspicious to Nitin, who has been eyeing me continuously, while the former will be too public.

Before I can fully make up my mind I find myself switching the car engine off in order to go to her. I let my instincts take over the show.

Just when I step out of the car my phone starts to buzz but without seeing who is calling I toss it into the car and plan to leave it there. I'm unbothered about anything else right now.

I daringly accost Aarti when she's reached the first building from her gate. It takes her a moment to register my presence when I politely obstruct her way. To say that she's startled when she sees me would be putting it mildly.

"**Nikhil**!... umm.. Hi... What are you doing here?" she says with too many pauses as she tries to accept the fact that despite her refusal I have come to meet her.

She's wearing an ordinary black vest with blue denims that accentuate her figure intoxicatingly. A blue sling bag hangs from her shoulder and black slippers cover her feet. Two jute bags with household items are held in either of her hands.

"Hi, Aarti," I grin, too excited to see her despite the obvious. I'm slightly embarrassed to be here but I feel none of the baggage that ideally I'm 'supposed' to feel when I meet Aarti. There's no guilt, no shame, nothing negative. It's almost as if a third person has introduced us and now I'm approaching her on my own; like what happened with Siddharth and Shreya. The only difference, of course, is that the third person in Sid's case is not his fiancée. Lucky him!

I sense the awkwardness that Aarti is bound to feel, now that we're face to face. I'm sure she must find it difficult to radiate the same vehemence towards me in person the way she did over the phone.

"What are you doing here?" she repeats herself, rooted to the spot. Strands of her just-tied-up hair have already come undone and gracefully border her face. She's just so simply beautiful, so plainly extraordinary that I'm already glad I came here. The elevation in my spirit just puts a stamp on my resolve and strengthens it further.

"I wanted to talk to you in person."

"Why?" she challenges. She doesn't say it in a derogatory or angry manner. Her tone shows that she's confused and hesitant rather than furious. She squints at me and puts both grocery bags in one hand.

"To explain myself. I didn't get a chance earlier."

"That's not true. You just didn't say anything when I was listening."

"You're right, I know. But it's hard to convey things. I can't afford anymore misunderstandings."

We're both mum for a few beats.

"Okay. Tell me…. Now that you're here, I might as well listen to this… Actually, it's been bothering me too much. Tell me," she says shifting from one foot to another. Curiosity spreads across her anxious face. She's not wearing any make-up at all, not even her trademark *kajal*. Her eyes seem washed out and tired.

"Here?" I ask, too conscious of our surroundings. I was hoping to talk to her at her place or if that's too uncomfortable, then any other place outside; definitely not here!

"Ya," she shrugs.

"Can we go to some place nearby?" I ask because I can't possibly ask her if I can come up to her place.

"**No,**" she says, sure of her answer. She's deliberately conversing in a monosyllabic way to convey her agitation.

"Why not? Please."

"Look, Nikhil, if you really have anything to say then just say it; though I highly doubt that anything can justify the nonsense that I had to hear," she says and puts both the grocery bags on the boot of the car right next to us.

I need to stop beating around the bush and come to the point. I've got the chance I wanted.

"Aarti... I ...look, I never told Neha that you seduced me or that you're coming in between us," I say, mortified. "Why would I say that when it's not true?"

I suddenly have a pressing need to urinate.

"I've heard all this, Nikhil. Why would Neha also lie like that then? Forget it. I guess it shall remain a mystery why Neha said all those disgusting things to me.....since she refuses to answer my calls and you don't seem to know either."

"No... it's not that. I know why she said... I mean...I think I know why."

Aarti's curiosity heightens. She implores me to go on.

"I'm just trying to make it clear that I haven't blamed you in any way for our break-up."

"It's clear," she says, running out of patience. Nitin passes by us, to and fro but doesn't seem to pry.

"I... I really like you, Aarti," I say quietly, in my smallest voice. My admission is nothing like the masculine, macho stuff that makes girls go weak in the knees. It's just a humble utterance of the truest words I've ever spoken.

She looks at me as if I've told her she's fat. I decide not to utter another word till she does. Then, possibly embarrassed by my remark, she totally ignores it and says, "Look, Nikhil…I… this conversation is just **wrong**. You being here, like this… Meeting me without Neha's knowledge… wait… she doesn't know right? That you're here?"

"No."

"This is wrong. You should go," she nods her disapproval. "I'm sorry that you guys are having problems. I don't know what to say," she admits looking at the ground beside my feet. She's behaving as if she actually did not hear what I said earlier. This must be so awkward for her.

"Aarti… you don't understand," I begin again and then suddenly, violently it starts to pour. Aarti dives into action, scooping her bags from the car, mouthing the word 'shit' and rushing to the protected space outside the lobby of Block A. At first I'm taken aback by the suddenness of the rain but then I remain fixed at my spot allowing it to drench me completely.

As soon as Aarti is out of the rain's field she abandons her bags on the side and fishes out her phone. After checking that it's okay she shoves it back in and looks at me. I stand motionless, observing her, wishing more than anything else to get soaked in this wrathful rain with her.

"**What are you doing!**" she hollers from where she stands, a few feet away from me. I shrug.

"Don't be stupid," she says gesturing me to come where she is. I comply.

I cautiously stand many steps away from her as numerous droplets glide off my sodden clothes. Then I gather her bags from the ground.

"Yuck! I hate getting wet in the rain," she says as a matter of fact. A few people in front of us run helter-skelter like Aarti just did. Then Nitin passes by, escorting an old lady to the gate under an umbrella. He looks at Aarti and says, "*Madam doh minute mein aata hoon.*"

"Thank you *bhaiya,*" she says gratefully. Then she turns to me.

"Nikhil, I think you should leave."

"Please. Let me finish what I have to say. You don't know anything yet. I won't rest till you do."

"But this... This is wrong, Nikhil. Don't misunderstand me. I'm very fond of you and no matter what Neha says, you both are still my friends. Whatever is going on between you two I hope it gets solved... but that's something you'll need to sort out on your own... and... and if there's any conversation **we** should have it should be in Neha's presence... **This**... This whole thing," she circulates her palms to gesticulate. "It's making me feel guilty for something I've not done... so please. I should go."

She takes her bags from me in one swift move and starts to walk when I reactively catch hold of her arm and say, "Aarti... I love you."

CHAPTER 33

Once again my insides feel pathetic. My whole body feels hot and bothered and even the rain cannot douse the ferocious fire inside me. The hollowness of my stomach has never been so pronounced and I feel utter weightlessness on confessing the cliché to Aarti.

She immediately wrenches her hand out of my grasp, making me feel like a gross, untouchable creature. Her face is contorted to an expression of sheer disgust.

"Are you **insane? Is this some sort of stupid joke**?" she roars. The way she speaks doesn't make the question sound rhetorical at all. She actually wants to know if I'm insane. Pure rage and astonishment mark her face and her breathing noticeably alters. I didn't expect her to say 'I love you too, Nikhil' but the degree of her wrath has me confounded. I'm slightly scared but still a hundred percent sure of what I've said.

I look away from her face to regain my composure and then look back at her. An eternity passes as I stare into bewildered, beautiful eyes. I just can't fathom what she's thinking.

She takes the odd silence between us as her cue and marches past me with hurried, purposeful steps. Then she's out of the parapet's protection and out in the rain. I immediately catch-up and hinder her path again.

"Wait. Please Aarti, say something. I know this is not what you expected. Give me a chance to make you understand. Please talk to me," I plead with her to put me out of my misery as the relentless rain unsparingly attacks us.

"Nikhil, I **refuse** to hear anything from you right now. Do you have **any idea** what you're **saying?** Just please move out of my way," she says trying a different track. I accost her again, now aware that we're playing cat and mouse in the open, though nobody is around us.

"Aarti, **please.** Don't walk away like this. Please can we go somewhere and talk where you won't run away. Can you **please please** do me this favour? I... I love you."

"**Stop it!**" she commands shutting both her ears with her hands as if hearing me is unbearable to her. "Just please stop talking!"

She looks almost comical with her grocery bags hanging from each hand beside her ears, and if it weren't for the situation we're in I would have wanted to laugh.

Before anything else can happen Nitin comes and stands next to us holding his gigantic, canopy-like umbrella that mainly protects Aarti. He looks at her, then at me, then back at her; then takes the grocery bags from her. "*Chale madam?*" he suggests, dutifully ready to usher her.

Staring me right in the eyes she tells Nitin, "*Haan chalo,*" and without another word she walks right past me. The two of them desert me as if I'm not standing there at all, and because of a third person's presence I'm unable to stop Aarti this time.

It takes almost a whole painful minute for my system to register what's happened. The vacuum Aarti leaves behind symbolises abandonment and emptiness to me which hurts almost literally. I feel despair and a fervent desperation; a desperation for her approval, a desperation for **her**. In spite of expecting this and knowing well that I would obviously have to come to terms with it, the actual rejection is unbearable to me. It's nothing I've ever experienced before, just like my feelings for Aarti. Suddenly, in the middle of this unknown surrounding, in this dismal atmosphere amongst total strangers I feel ostracised and everything around me seems surreal. How can something that did not exist in my world till a few days ago mean **so much** to me that the lack of it can make everything else seem meaningless? I have lived twenty-nine years in peace and contentment, independent and happy, unaware of this girl and her existence; but just after a few days of knowing her, how is it possible that **nothing** can bring me the happiness that I feel **she** can? The life I led before meeting her seems lacking. It makes **no** sense and yet here I am wasting away in the rain, literally washing my dirty linen in public.

Slowly, too slowly I walk up to my car feeling the same hollowness as before, but the weightlessness has been replaced by an unforgiving load. My body and my spirit feel broken. Everything has zoomed out of my attention but I subconsciously know that it's around.

I restlessly sit in the car, unbothered about making it wet and turn on the heater. It does nothing to change the cold ambience around me. It's not the cold we feel because of low temperatures but a cold and sterile emotion one would feel at a funeral or a hospital.

I will myself to snap out of this as I know that more problems await me, but none of those problems seem like problems anymore. I don't fear my parents' reaction, don't care if Neha tells them everything, and don't fear facing her parents. It's just not so important anymore. My full attention and devotion right now is to someone who's just walked away from me and sits a few floors above me. She's so close in proximity, just within my reach but seems more unreachable than ever. The more I deliberate on what's happening the more I regret existing at all.

Helpless, I start towards the main gate at the slowest possible speed of my life. The more inches I move away the more I feel like I'm leaving behind a huge piece of myself, a happiness that I'll never get my hands on again. It's too painful and emotionally exhausting. I reach the gate on a full brake and slight thud, and change my mind. It's like I needed this small jolt to awaken something within me. The gateman springs up from his seat to let me out and I automatically nod a 'no' to him, unaware but sure of what I'm doing.

I'm charged with a nameless energy and immediately make a very pronounced U-turn back into Aarti's building. I park in the same spot that I vacated only seconds ago and am now working at the opposite speed of moments ago. It's like I don't even know what's controlling me and yet I'm in total control. Paying no heed to my discarded phone I leave my car and prance the distance to her lobby, then approach the lift. Lucky for him, Nitin doesn't stop me this time.

Some nameless emotion is driving me totally insane. More than Aarti's refusal, which I can understand, it's her lack of acknowledgement of my love that's too unsettling. Possibly the shock of what she heard made her oblivious towards it, but that's not a bargain I'm willing to make. She can refuse my love, but she cannot deny that it exists. She can discard it from her life, because she never wanted it anyway, but she cannot disrespect it and render it invalid. I will not be at peace till Aarti genuinely realises, accepts and validates my feelings for her. After that she can do as per her will.

CHAPTER 34

It takes a minute for my bell to be answered.

"Nikhil, please just leave," Aarti's slightly distorted voice orders from behind the door between us. I suspect she's seen me through the keyhole.

"I will as soon as I've said what I have to. I won't leave till you hear me out, Aarti," I challenge her confidently. I just don't know what's taken over me but I know it stems from a primal need.

Without immediately realising how deranged this seems I persuade her to let me in again and again over the next five minutes, but she doesn't concede. When all my pleas fall on deaf ears I decide to take a stand, ironically, by sitting.

"Fine, I'll just sit here then," I warn her. "You'll have to open the door sometime, I'll wait here till then if that's what you want," I say because I mean it.

My behaviour is unexpected even to me and the irony of life is not lost on me. I never believed in this kind of love, simply because it seemed so impossible, so difficult and maybe because it had never happened to me. I didn't vigorously oppose it or anything, just felt that people deceived themselves into believing things like this; that dating and breaking-up is a vicious circle; that with time it's easy and possible to forget someone and move on with another. But as I sit on the floor outside Aarti's house I realise how easy and effortless it can be to love someone deeply and what it could take to forget someone we're madly in love with.

"**Why** are you doing this?" Aarti asks in a low, nervous voice probably after realising that I won't budge.

"I don't know, Aarti. I just need you to know; to understand."

We both let a moment pass. I begin again.

"You don't know me… and I'm being completely misunderstood. I wish you knew that I'm not like this, like how it's looking. It's just too important to me that you know everything the way it is…..the way it actually is…..not how it's looking right now. I …."

"But we don't even know each other, Nikhil. How does it matter? You're engaged to my best friend. Don't you realise that?"

"I do. Just please open the door, Aarti. You're talking to me anyway. Look…. You want me gone right? I'll go away right after I'm done. Just open the door once."

She doesn't respond and my spirits take a nosedive. How can I possibly convey the depth of my feelings if she refuses to even see my face? Should I just keep talking? It's actually the same thing. At least she's listening to me.

A few more hurtful moments pass.

"So, you really won't open the door for me?" I almost choke as I ask. This day has been thoroughly exhausting and I have no idea what's still keeping me going.

And then the click of the door makes my heart jump. I swirl in my spot and spring to my feet. Aarti stands in front of me, her door open, her expression wary, her clothes wet like mine. The two grocery bags she had lie discarded in the passageway behind her. They're a sopping mess despite their coarse texture and I feel slightly, foolishly, sorry about them.

Aarti stands motionless, wordless, her eyes avoiding mine. She stands granting my wish, awaiting my move; awaiting her rescue and relief once I leave. It's there again, that awkwardness, that embarrassment that I felt when we came face-to-face down in her building. A face, when added to a voice, can make such a difference. But I won't let her disarming presence throw me off balance this time.

"Thank you," I say politely and sense that she's slightly hesitant and frightened. Yep, she definitely thinks I'm a psycho. And considering what she has had to put up with, who can blame her?

"May I?" I ask as I put my right foot across the threshold of her house.

She nods a slight 'yes' and almost unwillingly shifts a little to let me in. I walk in. She swings the door behind me but doesn't completely shut it. The house is in pitch darkness, except for a single yellow spotlight that burns directly above us in the passageway. Two steps into the house and the kitchen appears on my right. Except the fridge which is right at the entrance, it's too dark to see anything else clearly. I turn to look at Aarti who stands close to the wall behind the door. She looks suspicious and distressed.

"You must be hating me by now, *na*?" I ask her sympathetically, confused whether I should sympathise with her or myself. A wistful smile involuntarily forms on my face. She just looks at the ground with the slightest movements every four seconds.

"I've troubled you so much today," I admit. She closes her eyes pointedly and clutches her forehead in her right palm, then folds her arms and looks down again. I try to inspect the house though I can see nothing clearly beyond the grocery bags.

"Nikhil," she calls me. "What will it take for you to just leave me alone right now?" she asks directly, unabashedly.

"You to acknowledge that I love you," I match her guts. "Accept it as a fact, as a reality. The way you... The way you looked at me when I told you. The way you disregarded it as if it's not there. Like it's not possible, it can't be.... like"

"Because **it can't!**" she cuts in. Her pitch conveys her frustration. "It can't be possible, Nikhil. There are certain boundaries and this is beyond them. It's unacceptable. And… and you don't even know me. How can you say such a big thing just like that? In the air? It's nonsense. What sort of escapism is this? Just because things are probably not working between you and Neha, how can you come to this conclusion?"

I control the rage I feel mentally and physically at her words. How **could** she say what she just said!

"This is abnormal; this crazy behaviour of yours. It's insanity. This is not love, it's rubbish," she says.

That's it! That does it for me. I lose all self-restraint as something almost unreal possesses me.

"How can you say that?" I screech. I stomp across the few steps between us, driven by an obsessive energy and almost drag her up the wall behind her. Both my hands pin both hers beside her head and she tries her best to wiggle out of my grasp, but in vain.

"How can **you** of all people say that?" I choke. A feral combination of fury and despair is taking over me. She arches her body towards me and pushes and struggles against my torso but I've lost all sense of right and wrong. I don't know what I'm doing but I don't stop talking.

"I can allow the **whole world** to say that. **The whole world.** I don't care what they say; **but you**? How can **you** say that I don't love you?" I demand. Her proximity is intoxicating. She's nothing less than a drug for me. My soaked body is pressed unforgivably against hers and I look right into the depths of her eyes as she tries to rid herself of me. I inhale her smell and it's my undoing.

"You… you don't know," I stifle a sob. "You don't even know Aarti. From the minute I saw you…. the first time… at my engagement. I haven't been able to think of anything else, anyone else. You've… you've taken over my whole world, my whole life. I think about you all the time, everyday. I remember everything you say, every single word. I remember everything you wear. I stare at your pictures all day. You're the only girl I've ever felt like this for; only girl I've ever been so obsessed with. And I don't even know why… or how… because like you said I don't even know you. But you

haven't left my mind from the first time I saw you. And....
and you say this is not **love**? I don't love you? How can you
say that?" I demand, willing her to understand me.

I'm out of my depth here as I passionately, obsessively tell
Aarti just how much I love her. I'm so absorbed in all my
emotions, so entranced by her proximity that I haven't
realised when Aarti stopped her physical protest against me.
She's not moving at all; her wrists aren't chaffing against
my palms, her body is not squirming against mine; she's
not demanding freedom from my embrace anymore. She's
listening to me intently, enraptured, spell-bound, staring
sincerely into my imploring eyes. I don't ease my grip and
don't break a second's eye-contact with her.

For the first time all evening I feel Aarti's not just hearing
my words but also listening to them. They're not just falling
on her ears, but also registering in her mind. It's **actually,
literally** reaching across to her how much I **love** her and
need her, as we breathlessly stare at each other. It's the most
beautiful moment I've ever lived. To be this connected with
her, not just physically but also emotionally is a euphoric,
almost out-of-body experience. It not only calms my nerves
but also soothes my soul. She **knows.** She **now** truly knows.

As I assert this in my mind I feel a freedom; an enigmatic
relief that I haven't felt since my engagement. I thought I
was incapable of feeling this way again. A dying hope re-
emerges in my mind. This girl is everything to me.

"I love you, Aarti. I want no one in this world except you."
I can tell that she's holding on to my **every** word, listening
and absorbing with wonder in her eyes, which are full of

questions, amazed at my revelations. I savour every moment in the seconds that pass and then my world falls apart.

Pools of unshed tears collect in Aarti's eyes and start to fall. Exuding no emotion, she sheds tear after tear which inexorably stream down her expressionless face and it sets alarm bells ringing in my whole system. The magnitude of what I've just done hits my conscience and I immediately release her, taking two steps back.

"Fuck."

It's like a switch inside my system was turned on, a monster unleashed and now the switch is off again.

"Aarti. Shit. I'm so sorry," I say in shock. "I'm so sorry. Shit. I didn't mean to do that. I didn't mean to scare you." The ugly truth of this seemingly charismatic moment with Aarti destroys all the exhilarating emotions I just witnessed, as it dawns on me how wrong my actions were. "I don't know what got into me. I'm sorry Aarti. Please forgive me," I plead.

She says nothing, emotes nothing; just stands absentmindedly rubbing her wrists against each other, staring at nothing in particular. Then she eases off the wall. There's a huge, wet imprint on it from her clothes. Her tears have stopped, been wiped off. I'm apologising profusely, randomly and she says nothing.

Then she opens the door that was ajar, turns to me and utters, "If you **don't** leave my house **right this moment, believe me,** I'll call security." Her tone is powerful and not to be argued with. I understand the extent of the gross damage I've done and that I must be prepared to face the repercussions. I say nothing more and do exactly as I'm told.

Once I'm out of the door and at the threshold of the elevator, I just can't resist glancing back. When I look back I don't see Aarti, just a door closing on me, closing this chapter for now.

CHAPTER 35

The journey back home is mostly a zombie-like, emotionless ride. Five unanswered calls, two from my mother and three from Siddharth await my attention but I don't return them immediately. I just mechanically drive home, unaffected, unperturbed and in some corner of my mind, ashamed of myself; ashamed because of my manhandling of Aarti. What I did was gross and borderline criminal. I need her to forgive me but I won't harass her for it. All I wanted from her was to be heard. Beyond that I can't do anything; can't extort any emotion from her whether it is love or forgiveness.

I'm slightly sated by the fact that she finally **knows** and keep reminding myself of it. Everything in my heart has been poured out. There are no lies, no secrets, and no guilt anymore. This is what it is.

I contemplate sending Aarti an apologetic message in order to ease my own conscience. I'm sorry that I misbehaved in order to express myself; not sorry that I love her. After some thought I decide against messaging. I must respect her decision to be left alone, let her digest the shocking fact that I love her, let her hate me for it.

I try to come to terms with the fact that this may be the end of the road for me; it's the outcome of the situation. It's more than likely that after today I may never have anything to do with Aarti or Neha in the reality of life. This unfortunate state of things right at this moment as I drive home could be the finality of the circumstance, and just as Neha can't force me to love her I can't force Aarti to love me.

It's not a very good feeling to acknowledge this but I take tremendous comfort in the fact that I've done all that I could to save the situation, sadly, by ruining it. It's a liberating and exhilarating sensation when you realise that you've done everything in your hands in order to achieve something, reach somewhere, and beyond this things are not in your control. Now it's nature's turn to play its role and I must surrender to its will.

ABOUT THE AUTHOR

A business graduate from Mumbai, Samah quit her job as a PR Executive to explore different career possibilities. She then worked for an events management company and has dabbled in modeling as well. The freedom of a freelance job gave her the time to discover her interests and it is in this period that she started to write her first story. During the process she realised her love for the art of storytelling and found that she has many a story to tell. She now regularly partakes in writing competitions and has been selected as the winner by author Preeti Shenoy for the Times of India short story competition.

Amongst other things, Samah is inclined towards a future in writing and hopes to encourage people to read and write even if they have other professional jobs. When she is not penning a manuscript she spends her time reading, watching movies, practising yoga, and baking. Traveling and trying various cuisines are big on her list of hobbies. She lives in Mumbai with her parents and three dogs.

www.ingramcontent.com/pod-product-compliance
Lightning Source LLC
Chambersburg PA
CBHW022202170626
46807CB00005B/2314